Familiar Quotations

Various

Contents

FAMILIAR QUOTATIONS

BY

Various

PREFACE.

The object of this work is to show, to some extent, the obligations our language owes to various authors for numerous phrases and familiar quotations which have become "household words."

This Collection, originally made without any view of publication, has been considerably enlarged by additions from an English work on a similar plan, and is now sent forth with the hope that it may be found a convenient book of reference.

Though perhaps imperfect in some respects, it is believed to possess the merit of accuracy, as the quotations have been taken from the original sources.

Should this be favorably received, endeavors will be made to make it more worthy of the approbation of the public in a future edition.

INDEX OF AUTHORS.

Byron, Lord
Campbell, Thomas
Canning, George
Carew, Thomas
Carey, Henry
Cervantes, Miguel de
Charles II
Churchill, Charles
Cibber, Colley
Coke, Lord
Coleridge, Samuel Taylor
Collins, William
Colman, George
Congreve, William
Cotton, Nathaniel
Cowley, Abraham
Cowper, William
Crabbe, George
Cranch, Christopher P.
Crashaw, Richard
Defoe, Daniel
Dekker, Thomas
Denham, Sir John
Doddridge, Philip
Dodsley, Robert
Donne, Dr. John
Drake, Joseph Rodman
Dryden, John
Dyer, John
Everett, David
Franklin, Benjamin
Fletcher, Andrew
Fouche, Joseph

Fuller, Thomas
Garrick, David
Gay, John
Goldsmith, Oliver
Grafton, Richard
Gray, Thomas
Green, Matthew
Greene, Albert G.
Greville, Fulke (Lord Brooke)
Halleck, Fitz-Greene
Herbert, George
Herrick, Robert
Hervey, Thomas K.
Hill, Aaron
Hobbes, Thomas
Holy Scriptures
Holmes, Oliver Wendell
Home, John
Hood, Thomas
Hopkinson, Joseph
Irving, Washington
Johnson, Samuel
Jones, Sir William
Jonson, Ben
Keats, John
Key, F.S.
Kempis, Thomas a
Lamb, Charles
Langhorn, John
Lee, Nathaniel
L'Estrange, Roger
Longfellow, Henry Wadsworth
Lowell, James Russell

Lovelace, Sir Richard
Lyttelton, Lord
Lytton, Edward Bulwer
Macaulay, Thomas Babington
Marlowe, Christopher
Mickle, William Julius
Milnes, Richard Monckton
Milton, John,
Montague, Lady Mary Wortley
Montrose, Marquis of
Moore, Edward
Moore, Thomas
Morris, Charles
Morton, Thomas
Moss, Thomas
Norris, John
Otway, Thomas
Paine, Thomas
Palafox, Don Joseph
Parnell, Thomas
Percy, Thomas
Philips, John
Pollok, Robert
Pope, Alexander
Porteus, Beilby
Prior, Matthew
Proctor, Bryan Walter
Quarles, Francis
Rabelais, Francis
Raleigh, Sir Walter
Randolph, John
Rochefoucauld, Duc de
Rochester, Earl of

Rogers, Samuel
Roscommon, Earl of
Rowe, Nicholas
Savage, Richard
Scott, Sir Walter
Sewall, Jonathan M.
Sewell, Dr. George
Shakespeare, William
Sheffield, Duke of Buckinghamshire
Shenstone, William
Sheridan, Richard Brinsley
Shirley, James
Sidney, Sir Philip
Smollett, Tobias
Southern, Thomas
Southey, Robert
Spencer, William R.
Spenser, Edmund
Sprague, Charles
Steers, Miss Fanny
Sterne, Laurence
Suckling, Sir John
Swift, Jonathan
Sylvester, Joshua
Taylor, Henry
Tennyson, Alfred
Tertullian
Theobald, Louis
Thomson, James
Thrale, Mrs
Tickell, Thomas
Trumbull, John
Tuke, Sir Samuel

Tusser, Thomas
Uhland, John Louis
Walcott John (Peter Pindar)
Waller, Edmund
Warburton, Thomas
Watts, Isaac
Wither, George
Wolfe, Charles
Woodsworth, Samuel
Wordsworth, William
Wotton, Sir Henry
Young, Edward

A COLLECTION OF FAMILIAR QUOTATIONS

HOLY SCRIPTURES.

OLD TESTAMENT.

Genesis ii. 18.

It is not good that the man should be alone

Genesis iii. 19.

For dust thou art, and unto dust shalt thou return.

Genesis iv. 9.

Am I my brother's keeper?

Genesis iv. 13.

My punishment is greater than I can bear

Genesis ix. 6.

Whoso sheddeth man's blood, by man shall his blood be shed.

Genesis xvi. 12.

His hand will be against every man, and every man's hand against him.

Genesis xlii. 38.

Bring down my gray hairs with sorrow to the grave.

Genesis xlix. 4.

Unstable as water, thou shalt not excel.

Deuteronomy xix. 21.

Eye for eye, tooth for tooth, hand for hand, foot for foot.

Deuteronomy xxxii. 10.

He kept him as the apple of his eye.

Judges xvi. 9.

The Philistines be upon thee, Samson.

Ruth i. 16.

For whither thou goest, I will go; and where thou lodgest, I will lodge: thy people shall be my people, and thy God my God.

Samuel xiii. 14.

A man after his own heart.

Samuel i. 20.

Tell it not in Gath; publish it not in the streets of Ashkelon

Samuel i. 23.

Saul and Jonathan were lovely and pleasant in their lives, and in their death they were not divided.

Samuel i. 25.

How are the mighty fallen in the midst of the battle!

Samuel i. 26.

Very pleasant hast thou been unto me: thy love to me was wonderful, passing the love of women.

Samuel xii. 7.

And Nathan said to David, Thou art the man.

Kings ix, 7.

A proverb and a by-word among all people,

Kings xviii. 21.

How long halt ye between two opinions?

Kings xviii. 44.

Behold, there ariseth a little cloud out of the sea, like a man's hand.

Kings xix. 12.

A still, small voice.

Kings xx. 11.

Let not him that girdeth on his harness boast himself as he that putteth it off.

Kings iv. 40.

There is death in the pot.

Job i. 21.

The Lord gave, and the Lord hath taken away; blessed be the name of the Lord.

Job iii. 17.

There the wicked cease from troubling, and there the weary be at rest.

Job v. 7.

Yet man is born unto trouble, as the sparks fly upward.

Job xvi. 2.

Miserable comforters are ye all.

Job xix. 25.

I know that my Redeemer liveth.

Job xxviii. 18.

The price of wisdom is above-rubies.

Job xxix. 15.

I was eyes to the blind, and feet was I to the lame.

Job xxxi. 35.

That mine adversary had written a book.

Job xxxviii. 11.

Hitherto shalt thou come, but no further; and here shall thy proud waves be stayed.

Psalm xvi. 6.

The lines are fallen unto me in pleasant places.

Psalm xviii. 10.

Yea, he did fly upon the wings of the wind.

Psalm xxiii. 2.

He maketh me to lie down in green pastures he leadeth me beside the still waters.

Psalm xxiii. 4.

Thy rod and thy staff they comfort me.

Psalm xxxvii. 25.

I have been young, and now am old; yet have I not seen the righteous forsaken, nor his seed begging bread.

Psalm xxxvii. 35.

Spreading himself like a green bay tree.

Psalm xxxvii. 37.

Mark the perfect man, and behold the upright.

Psalm xxxix. 3.

While I was musing the fire burned.

Psalm xlv. 1.

My tongue is the pen of a ready writer.

Psalm lv. 6.

Oh, that I had wings like a dove!

Psalm lxxii. 9.

His enemies shall lick the dust.

Psalm lxxxv. 10.

Mercy and truth are met together: righteousness and peace have kissed each other.

Psalm xc. 9.

We spend our years as a tale that is told.

Psalm cvii. 27.

They reel to and fro, and stagger like a drunken man, and are at their wit's end.

Psalm cxxvii. 2.

He giveth his beloved sleep.

Psalm cxxxiii. 1.

Behold, how good and how pleasant it is for brethren to dwell together in unity!

Psalm cxxxvii. 5.

If I forget thee, O Jerusalem, let my right hand forget her cunning.

Psalm cxxxvii. 2.

We hanged our harps on the willows.

Psalm cxxxix. 14.

For I am fearfully and wonderfully made.

Proverbs iii. 17.

Her ways are ways of pleasantness, and all her paths are peace.

Proverbs xi. 14.

In the multitude of counsellors there is safety.

Proverbs xiii. 12.

Hope deferred maksth the heart sick.

Proverbs xiv. 9.

Fools make a mock at sin.

Proverbs xiv. 10.

The heart knoweth his own bitterness.

Proverbs xiv. 34.

Righteousness exalteth a nation.

Proverbs xv. 1.

A soft answer turneth away wrath.

Proverbs xv. 17.

Better is a dinner of herbs where love is, than a stalled ox and hatred therewith.

Proverbs xvi. 18.

Pride goeth before destruction, and a haughty spirit before a fall.

Proverbs xvi. 31.

The hoary head is a crown of glory.

Proverbs xviii. 14.

A wounded spirit who can bear?

Proverbs xxii. 6.

Train up a child in the way he should go; and when he is old he will not depart from it.

Proverbs xxiii. 5.

For riches certainly make themselves wings.

Proverbs xxiv. 33.

Yet a little sleep, a little slumber, a little folding of the hands to sleep.

Proverbs xxv. 22.

For thou shalt heap coals of fire upon his head.

Proverbs xxvi. 13.

There is a lion in the way; a lion is in the streets.

Proverbs xxvii. 1.

Boast not thyself of to-morrow; for thou knowest not what a day may bring forth.

Proverbs xxviii. 1.

The wicked flee when no man pursueth.

Ecclesiastes i. 9.

There is no new thing under the sun.

Ecclesiastes i. 14.

All is vanity and vexation of spirit.

Ecclesiastes v. 12.

The sleep of a laboring man is sweet.

Ecclesiastes vii. 2.

It is better to go to the house of mourning than to go to the house of feasting.

Ecclesiastes vii. 16.

Be not righteous overmuch

Ecclesiastes ix. 4.

For a living dog is better than a dead lion,

Ecclesiastes ix. 10.

Whatsoever thy hand findeth to do, do it with thy might.

Ecclesiastes ix. 11.

The race is not to the swift, nor the battle to the strong.

Ecclesiastes xi. 1.

Cast thy bread upon the waters; for thou shalt find it after many days.

Ecclesiastes xii. 1.

Remember now thy Creator in the days of thy youth.

Ecclesiastes xii. 5.

And the grasshopper shall be a burden.

Ecclesiastes xii. 5.

Man goeth to his long home.

Ecclesiastes xii. 6.

Or ever the silver cord be loosed, or the golden bowl be broken, or the pitcher be broken at the fountain, or the wheel broken at the cistern.

Ecclesiastes xii. 7.

Then shall the dust return to the earth as it was; and the spirit shall return unto God who gave it.

Ecclesiastes xii. 8.

Vanity of vanities, saith the Preacher; all is vanity.

Ecclesiastes xii. 12.

Of making many books there is no end; and much study is a weariness of the flesh.

Isaiah xi. 6.

The wolf also shall dwell with the lamb, and the leopard shall lie down with the kid.

Isaiah xxviii. 10.

Precept upon precept; line upon line: here a little, and there a little.

Isaiah xxxviii. 1.

Set thine house in order.

Isaiah xl. 6.

All flesh is grass.

Isaiah xl. 15.

Behold, the nations are as a drop of a bucket, and are counted as the small dust of the balance.

Isaiah xlii. 3.

A bruised reed shall he not break, and the smoking flax shall he not quench.

Isaiah liii. 7.

He is brought as a lamb to the slaughter.

Isaiah lx. 22.

A little one shall become a thousand, and a small one a strong nation.

Isaiah lxi. 3.

To give unto them beauty for ashes, the oil of joy for mourning, the garment of praise for the spirit of heaviness.

Isaiah lxiv. 6.

We all do fade as a leaf.

Jeremiah vii. 3.

Amend your ways and your doings.

Jeremiah viii. 22.

Is there no balm in Gilead? is there no physician there?

Jeremiah xiii. 23.

Can the Ethiopian change his skin, or the leopard his spots?

Ezekiel xviii. 2.

The fathers have eaten sour grapes, and the children's teeth are set on edge.

Daniel v. 27.

Thou art weighed in the balances, and art found wanting.

Daniel vi. 12.

The thing is true, according to the law of the Medes and Persians, which altereth not.

Hosea viii. 7.

For they have sown the wind, and they shall reap the whirlwind.

Micah iv. 3.

And they shall beat their swords into plough-shares, and their spears into pruning-hooks.

Micah iv. 4.

But they shall sit every man under his vine and under his fig tree.

Habakkuk ii. 2.

Write the vision, and make it plain upon tables, that he may run that readeth it.

Malachi iv. 2.

But unto you that fear my name shall the Sun of righteousness arise with healing in his wings.

Ecelesiasticus xiii. 1.

He that toucheth pitch shall be defiled therewith.

Ecelesiasticus xiii. 7.

He will laugh thee to scorn.

COMMON PRAYER.

Morning Prayer.

We have left undone those things which we ought to have done; and we have done those things which we ought not to have done.

Psalm cv. 18.

The iron entered into his soul. Collect for the Second Sunday in Advent. Read, mark, learn, and inwardly digest.

The Burial Service.

In the midst of life we are in death. Earth to earth, ashes to ashes, dust to dust.

NEW TESTAMENT.

Matthew ii. 18.

Rachel weeping for her children, and would not be comforted, because they are not.

Matthew iv. 4.

Man shall not live by bread alone.

Matthew v. 13.

Ye are the salt of the earth: but if the salt have lost his savor, wherewith shall it be salted?

Matthew v. 14.

Ye are the light of the world. A city set upon a hill cannot be hid.

Matthew vi. 3.

But when thou doest alms, let not thy left hand know what thy right hand doeth.

Matthew vi. 21.

Where your treasure is, there will your heart be also.

Matthew vi. 24.

Ye cannot serve God and Mammon.

Matthew vi. 28.

Consider the lilies of the field, how they grow; they toil not, neither do they spin.

Matthew vi. 34.

Take therefore no thought for the morrow; for the morrow shall take thought for the things of itself. Sufficient unto the day is the evil thereof.

Matthew vii. 6.

Neither cast ye your pearls before swine.

Matthew vii. 7.

Ask, and it shall be given you; seek, and ye shall find; knock, and it shall be opened unto you.

Matthew viii. 20.

The foxes have holes, and the birds of the air have nests; but the Son of Man hath not where to lay his head.

Matthew ix. 37.

The harvest truly is plenteous, but the laborers are few.

Matthew x. 16.

Be ye therefore wise as serpents, and harmless as doves.

Matthew x. 30.

But the very hairs of your head are all numbered.

Matthew xii. 33.

The tree is known by his fruit.

Matthew xii. 34.

Out of the abundance of the heart the mouth speaketh.

Matthew xiii. 57.

A prophet is not without honor, save in his own country, and in his own house.

Matthew xiv. 27.

Be of good cheer: it is I; be not afraid.

Matthew xv. 14.

And if the blind lead the blind, both shall fall into the ditch.

Matthew xv. 27.

Yet the dogs eat of the crumbs which fall from their masters' table.

Matthew xvi. 23.

Get thee behind me, Satan.

Matthew xvi. 26.

For what is a man profited, if he shall gain the whole world, and lose his own soul?

Matthew xvii. 4.

It is good for us to be here.

Matthew xix. 6.

What therefore God hath joined together let not man put asunder.

Matthew xix. 24.

It is easier for a camel to go through the eye of a needle than for a rich man to enter into the kingdom of God.

Matthew xx. 15.

Is it not lawful for me to do what I will with mine own?

Matthew xxii. 14.

For many are called, but few are chosen.

Matthew xxiii. 24.

Ye blind guides! which strain at a gnat, and swallow a camel.

Matthew xxiii. 27.

For ye are like unto whited sepulchres, which indeed appear beautiful outward, but are within full of dead men's bones.

Matthew xxiv. 28.

For wheresoever the carcass is, there will the eagles be gathered together.

Matthew xxv. 29.

Unto every one that hath shall be given, and he shall have abundance: but from him that hath not shall be taken away even that which he hath.

Matthew xxvi. 41.

Watch and pray, that ye enter not into temptation: the spirit indeed is willing, but the flesh is weak.

Mark iv. 9.

He that hath ears to hear, let him hear.

Mark v. 9.

My name is Legion.

Mark ix. 44.

Where their worm dieth not, and the fire is not quenched.

Luke iii. 9.

And now also the ax is laid unto the root of the trees.

Luke iv. 23.

Physician, heal thyself.

Luke x. 37.

Go, and do thou likewise.

Luke x. 42.

But one thing is needful: and Mary hath chosen that good part, which shall not be taken away from her.

Luke xi. 23.

He that is not with me is against me.

Luke xii. 19.

And I will say to my soul, Soul, thou hast much goods laid up for many years; take thine ease, eat, drink, and be merry.

Luke xii. 35.

Let your loins be girded about, and your lights burning.

Luke xvi. 8.

For the children of this world are in their generation wiser than the children of light.

Luke xvii. 2.

It were better for him that a millstone were hanged about his neck, and he cast into the sea.

Luke xvii. 32.

Remember Lot's wife.

Luke xix. 22.

Out of thine own mouth will I judge thee.

John i. 29.

Behold the Lamb of God, which taketh away the sin of the world!

John i. 46.

Can there any good thing come out of Nazareth?

John iii. 3.

Except a man be born again, he cannot see the kingdom of God.

John iii. 8.

The wind bloweth where it listeth.

John v. 35. He was a burning and a shining light.

John vi. 12.

Gather up the fragments that remain, that nothing be lost.

John vii. 24.

Judge not according to the appearance.

John xii. 8.

For the poor always ye have with you.

John xii, 35.

Walk while ye have the light, lest darkness come upon you.

John xiv. 1.

Let not your heart be troubled.

John xiv. 2.

In my Father's house are many mansions.

John xv. 13.

Greater love hath no man than this, that a man lay down his life for his friends.

Acts ix. 5.

It is hard for thee to kick against the pricks.

Acts xx. 35.

It is more blessed to give than to receive.

Romans ii. 11.

For there is no respect of persons with God.

Romans vi. 23.

For the wages of sin is death.

Romans viii. 28.

And we know that all things work together or good to them that love God.

Romans xii. 16.

Be not wise in your own conceits.

Romans xii. 20.

Therefore if thine enemy hunger, feed him; if he thirst, give him drink:

for in so doing thou shalt heap coals of fire on his head.

Romans xii. 21.

Be not overcome of evil, but overcome evil with good.

Romans xiii. 1.

The powers that be are ordained of God,

Romans xiii. 7.

Render therefore to all their dues.

Romans xiii. 10.

Love is the fulfilling of the law.

Romans xiv. 5.

Let every man be fully persuaded in his own mind.

1 Corinthians iii. 6.

I have planted, Apollos watered; but God gave the increase.

1 Corinthians iii. 13.

Every man's work shall be made manifest,

1 Corinthians v. 3.

Absent in body, but present in spirit.

1 Corinthians v. 6.

Know ye not that a little leaven leaveneth the whole lump?

1 Corinthians vii. 31.

For the fashion of this world passeth away,

1 Corinthians ix. 22.

I am made all things to all men.

1 Corinthians x. 12.

Wherefore let him that thinketh he standeth take heed lest he fall.

1 Corinthians xiii. 1.

As sounding brass, or a tinkling cymbal.

1 Corinthians xiii. 11.

When I was a child I spake as a child.

1 Corinthians xiii. 12.

For now we see through a glass, darkly.

1 Corinthians xv. 33.

Be not deceived: evil communications corrupt good manners.

1 Corinthians xv. 47.

The first man is of the earth, earthy.

1 Corinthians xv. 55.

O death, where is thy sting? O grave, where is thy victory?

2 Corinthians v. 7.

We walk by faith, not by sight.

2 Corinthians vi. 2.

Behold, now is the accepted time,

2 Corinthians vi. 8.

By evil report and good report.

Galatians vi. 5.

For every man shall bear his own burden,

Galatians vi. 7.

Whatsoever a man soweth, that shall he also reap.

Ephesians iv. 26.

Be ye angry, and sin not: let not the sun go down upon your wrath.

Philippians i. 21.

For to me to live is Christ, and to die is gain.

Colossians ii. 21.

Touch not; taste not; handle not.

1 Thessalonians i. 3.

Remembering without ceasing your work of faith, and labor of love.

1 Thessalonians v. 21.

Prove all things; hold fast that which is good.

1 Timothy iii. 3,

Not greedy of filthy lucre.

1 Timothy v. 18.

The laborer is worthy of his reward.

1 Timothy v. 23.

Drink no longer water, but use a little wine for thy stomach's sake.

1 Timothy vi. 10.

For the love of money is the root of all evil.

2 Timothy iv. 7.

I have fought a good fight, I have finished my course, I have kept the faith.

Titus i. 15.

Unto the pure all things are pure.

Hebrews xi. 1.

Now faith is the substance of things hoped' for, the evidence of things not seen.

Hebrews xii. 6.

For whom the Lord loveth he chasteneth.

Hebrews xiii. 2.

Be not forgetful to entertain strangers, for thereby some have entertained angels unawares.

James i. 12.

Blessed is the man that endureth temptation for when he is tried he shall receive the crown of life.

James iii. P

Behold, how great a matter a little fire kindleth!

James iv. 7.

Resist the devil, and he will flee from you.

1 Peter iv. 8.

Charity shall cover the multitude of sins.

1 Peter v. 8.

Be sober, be vigilant; because your adversary the devil, as a roaring lion, walketh about seeking whom he may devour.

2 Peter iii. 10.

But the day of the Lord will come as a thief in the night.

1 John iv. 18.

There is no fear in love; but perfect love casteth out fear.

Revelation ii. 10.

Be thou faithful unto death.

Revelation ii. 27.

He shall rule them with a rod of iron.

Revelation xxii. 13.

I am Alpha and Omega, the beginning and the end, the first and the last.

SHAKESPEARE.

TEMPEST.

Act i. Sc. 2.

There's nothing ill can dwell in such a
temple:
If the ill spirit have so fair a house,
Good things will strive to dwell with 't.

Act i. Sc. 2.

I will be correspondent to command,
And do my spiriting gently.

Act ii. Sc. 2.

A very ancient and fishlike smell.

Act ii. Sc. 2.

Misery acquaints a man with strange bed-fellows.

Act iv. Sc. 1.

Our revels row are ended: these our actors,
As I foretold you, were all spirits, and
Are melted into air, into thin air:
And, like the baseless fabric of this vision,
The cloud-capped towers, the gorgeous palaces,
The solemn temples, the great globe itself
Yea, all which it inherit, shall dissolve,
And, like an insubstantial pageant faded,
Leave not a rack behind.

Act iv. Sc. 1.

We are such stuff
As dreams are made of, and our little life
Is rounded with a sleep.

TWO GENTLEMEN OF VERONA.

Act i. Sc. 2.

I have no other but a woman's reason;

I think him so, because I think him so.

Act iv. Sc. 1.

To make a virtue of necessity.

Act iv. Sc. 4.

Is she not passing fair?

MERRY WIVES OF WINDSOR.

Act ii. Sc. 1.

Faith, thou hast some crotchets in thy head now.

Act ii. Sc. 2.

Why, then the world's mine oyster,
Which I with sword will open.

Act v. Sc. 1.

They say, there is divinity in odd numbers,
either in nativity, chance, or death.

TWELFTH NIGHT.

Act i. Sc. 1.

If music be the food of love, play on,
Give me excess of it; that, surfeiting,
The appetite may sicken, and so die.--
That strain again--it had a dying fall;
O, it came o'er my ear like the sweet south,
That breathes upon a bank of violets,
Stealing and giving odor.

Act i. Sc, 3.

I am sure care's an enemy to life.

Act i. Sc. 5.

'Tis beauty truly blent, whose red and white
Nature's own sweet and cunning hand laid on.

Act ii. Sc. 3.

Dost thou think, because them art virtuous,
there shall be no more cakes and ale?

Act ii. Sc. 4.

She never told her love,
But let concealment, like a worm in the bud,
Feed on her damask cheek: she pined in thought,
And, with a green and yellow melancholy,
She sat, like Patience on a monument,
Smiling at grief.

Act iii. Sc. 1.

O, what a deal of scorn looks beautiful
In the contempt and anger of his lip!

Act iii. Sc. 1.

Love sought is good, but given unsought is
better.

Act iii. Sc, 2.

Let there be gall enough in thy ink; though
thou write with a goose-pen, no matter.

Act iii. Sc. 4.

Some are born great, some achieve greatness,
and some have greatness thrust upon them.

MEASURE FOR MEASURE.

Act i. Sc. 1.

Spirits are not finely touched
But to fine issues.

Act i. Sc. 5.

Our doubts are traitors,
And make us lose the good we oft might win,
By fearing to attempt.

Act ii. Sc. 2.

O, it is excellent
To have a giant's strength; but it is tyrannous
To use it like a giant.

Act ii. Sc. 2.

But man, proud man!
Drest in a little brief authority,
Plays such fantastic tricks before high Heaven
As make the angels weep.

Act iii. Sc. 1.

The miserable have no other medicine,
But only hope.

Act iii. Sc. 1.

The sense of death is most in apprehension;
And the poor beetle that we tread upon
In corporal sufferance finds a pang as great
As when a giant dies.

Act iii. Sc. 1.

Ay, but to die, and go we know not where;
To lie in cold obstruction, and to rot.

Act iv. Sc. 1.

Take, O take those lips away,
That so sweetly were forsworn;
And those eyes, the break of day,
Lights that do mislead the morn;
But my kisses bring again,
Seals of love, but sealed in vain.[1]

[Note 1: This song; is found in "The Bloody Brother, or Rollo, Duke
of Normandy," by Beaumont and Fletcher, Act 5, Sc. 2, with the following
additional stanza:

"Hide, O hide those hills of snow,
Which thy frozen bosom bears,
On whose tops the fruits that grow
Are of those that April wears;
But first set my poor heart free.
Bound in those icy chains for thee."

There has been much controversy about the authorship, but the more probable opinion seems to be that the second stanza was added by Fletcher.]

MUCH ADO ABOUT NOTHING.

Act i. Sc. 1.

He hath indeed better bettered expectation.

Act ii. Sc. 1.

Friendship is constant in all other things,
Save in the office and affairs of love.
Therefore, all hearts in love use their own tongues;
Let every eye negotiate for itself,
And trust no other agent.

Act ii. Sc. 1.

Silence is the perfectest herald of joy; I were but little happy, if I could say how much.

Act ii. Sc. 3.

Sits the wind in that corner?

Act ii. Sc. 3.

When I said I should die a bachelor, I did not think I should live till I were married.

Act iii. Sc. 1.

Some, Cupid kills with arrows, some with traps.

Act iii. Sc. 2.

Everyone can master a grief, but he that Lath it.

Act iii. Sc. 3.

Are you good men and true?

Act iii. Sc. 3.

Is most tolerable, and not to be endured.

Act iii. Sc. 4.

Comparisons are odorous.

Act iv. Sc. 2.

O that he were here to write me down--an ass!

Act iv. Sc. 2.

A fellow that had losses.

Act v. Sc. 1.

For there was never yet philosopher
That could endure the toothache patiently.

MIDSUMMER NIGHT'S DREAM.

Act i. Sc. 1.

But earthly happier is the rose distilled
Than that which, withering on the virgin thorn
Grows, lives, and dies in single blessedness.

Act i. Sc. 1.

Ah me! for aught that ever I could read,
Could ever hear by tale or history,
The course of true love never did run smooth.

Act i. Sc. 1.

Love looks not with the eyes, but with the mind;
And therefore is winged Cupid painted blind.

Act i. Sc. 2.

A proper man as any one shall see in a summer's day.

Act ii. Sc. 2.

In maiden meditation, fancy free.

Act ii. Sc. 2.

I'll put a girdle round about the earth
In forty minutes.

Act ii. Sc. 2.

I know a bank whereon the wild thyme blows,
Where ox-lips and the nodding violet grows.

Act iii. Sc. 2.

So we grew together,
Like to a double cherry, seeming parted.

Act v. Sc. 1.

The poet's eye, in a fine frenzy rolling,
Doth glance from heaven to earth, from earth to heaven,
And as imagination bodies forth
The forms of things unknown, the poet's pen
Turns them to shape, and gives to airy nothing
A local habitation and a name.

LOVE'S LABOR'S LOST.

Act ii. Sc. 1.

A merrier man,
Within the limit of becoming mirth,
I never spent an hour's talk withal.

Act v. Sc. 1.

He draweth the thread of his verbosity finer than the staple of his
argument.

MERCHANT OF VENICE.

Act i. Sc. 1.

I hold the world but as the world, Gratiano;
A stage, where every man must play a part,
And mine a sad one.

Act i. Sc. 1.

Why should a man, whose blood is warm
within,
Sit like his grandsire cut in alabaster?

Act i. Sc. 1.

I am Sir Oracle,
And when I ope my lips, let no dog bark!

Act i, Sc. 1.

Gratiano speaks an infinite deal of nothing; more than any man in all
Venice. His reasons are as two grains of wheat hid in two bushels of
chaff: you shall seek all day ere you find them: and, when you have
them, they are not worth the search.

Act i. Sc. 3.

Even there, where merchants most do congregate.

Act i. Sc. 3.

The devil can cite Scripture for his purpose.

Act i. Sc. 3.

Sufferance is the badge of all our tribe,

Act i. Sc. 3.

Many a time, and oft,
the Rialto, have you rated me.

Act ii. Sc. 2.

It is a wise father that knows his own child.

Act ii, Sc. 6.

All things that are,
Are with more spirits chased than enjoyed.

Act ii. Sc. 7.

All that glisters is not gold.

Act iii. Sc. 1.

I am a Jew: hath not a Jew eyes? hath not
a Jew hands, organs, dimensions, senses,
affections, passions?

Act iii. Sc. 5.

Thus when I shun Scylla, your father, I fall
into Charybdis, your mother.

Act iv. Sc. 1.

What! wouldst thou have a serpent sting
thee twice?

Act iv. Sc. 1.

The quality of mercy is not strained;
It droppeth, as the gentle rain from heaven
Upon the place beneath: it is twice blessed;
It blesseth him that gives, and him that takes,

Act iv. Sc. 1.

A Daniel come to judgment.

Act iv. Sc. 1.

Is it so nominated in the bond.
I cannot find it; 'tis not in the bond?

Act iv. Sc. 1.

I have thee on the hip

Act iv. Sc. 1.

I thank thee, Jew, for teaching me that word

Act v. Sc. 1.

How sweet the moonlight sleeps upon this bank!

Act v. Sc. 1.

I am never merry when I hear sweet music.

Act v. Sc. 1.

The man that hath no music in himself,

Nor is not moved with concord of sweet sounds,
Is fit for treasons, stratagems, and spoils.

Act v. Sc. 1.

How far that little candle throws his beams!
So shines a good deed in a naughty world.

AS YOU LIKE IT.

Act i. Sc. 2.

Well said: that was laid on with a trowel.

Act i. Sc. 2.

My pride fell with my fortunes.

Act i. Sc. 3.

Cel. Not a word?
Ros. Not one to throw at a dog.

Act i. Sc. 3.

O how full of briers is this working-day world!

Act ii. Sc. 1.

Sweet are the uses of adversity,
Which, like the toad, ugly and venomous,
Wears yet a precious jewel in his head.

Act ii. Sc. 1.

And this our life, exempt from public haunts,
Finds tongues in trees, books in the running brooks,
Sermons in stones, and good in everything.

Act ii. Sc. 1.

"Poor deer," quoth he, "thou mak'st a testament,
As wordlings do, giving thy sum of more
To that which had too much."

Act ii. Sc. 3.

And He that doth the ravens feed,
Yea, providently caters for the sparrow,
Be comfort to my age!

Act ii. Sc. 3.

For in my youth I never did apply
Hot and rebellious liquors in my blood;
Therefore my age is as a lusty winter,

Frosty, but kindly.

Act ii. Sc. 7.

And railed on lady Fortune in good terms,
In good set terms....
And looking on it with lack-luster eye,
"Thus we may see," quoth he, "how the
world wags.
And so from hour to hour we ripe and ripe,
And then from hour to hour we rot and rot,
And thereby hangs a tale."
Motley's the only wear.

Act ii. Sc. 7.

If ladies be but young and fair,
They have the gift to know it.

Act ii. Sc. 7.

I must have liberty
Withal, as large a charter as the wind,
To blow on whom I please.

Act ii. Sc. 7.

The why is plain as way to parish church.

Act ii. Sc. 7.

All the world's a stage
And all the men and women merely players:
They have their exits and their entrances,
And one man in his time plays many parts
And then, the whining schoolboy, with his satchel,
And shining morning face, creeping like snail
Unwillingly to school. And then, the lover,
Sighing like furnace, with a woeful ballad
Made to his mistress' eyebrow. Then, a soldier,
Full of strange oaths, and bearded like the pard,
Jealous in honor, sudden and quick in quarrel,
Seeking the bubble reputation
Even in the cannon's mouth And then the justice,
Full of wise saws and modern instances,
And so he plays his part. The sixth age shifts
Into the lean and slippered pantaloon.
Last scene of all,
That ends this strange, eventful history,
Is second childishness, and mere oblivion.

Act ii. Sc. 7.

Blow, blow, thou winter wind,
Thou art not so unkind
As man's ingratitude.

Act iii. Sc. 2.

Hast any philosophy in thee, shepherd?

Act iii. Sc. 8.

Truly, I would the gods had made thee poetical.

Act iv. Sc. 1.

I had rather have a fool to make me merry, than experience to make me sad.

Act iv. Sc. 1.

Men have died from time to time, and worms have eaten them, but not for love.

Act iv. Sc. 3.

Pacing through the forest,
Chewing the food of sweet and bitter fancy.

Act v. Sc. 2.

How bitter a thing it is to look into happiness through another man's eyes!

Act v. Sc. 4.

Your *If* is the only peacemaker; much
virtue in *If*.

Epilogue.

Good wine needs no bush.

TAMING OF THE SHREW.

Act iv. Sc. 1,

And thereby hangs a tale.

Act v. Sc. 2.

My cake is dough.

WINTER'S TALE.

Act iv. Sc. 2.

A merry heart goes all the day,
Your sad tires in a mile-a.

Act iv. Sc. 3.

Daffodils,
That come before the swallow dares, and take

The winds of March with beauty; violets, dim,
But sweeter than the lids of Juno's eyes,
Or Cytherea's breath.

Act iv. Sc. 3.

When you do dance, I wish you
A wave o' the sea, that you might ever do
Nothing but that.

ALL'S WELL THAT ENDS WELL.

Act i. Sc. 1.

It were all one,
That I should love a bright, particular star,
And think to wed it, he is so above me.

Act v. Sc. 3.

Praising what is lost
Makes the remembrance dear.

COMEDY OF ERRORS.

Act v. Sc. 1.

They brought one Pinch, a hungry, lean-faced villain,
A mere anatomy.

MACBETH.

Act i. Sc. 1.

When shall we three meet again,
In thunder, lightning, or in rain?

Act i. Sc. 1.

Fair is foul, and foul is fair.

Act i. Sc. 3.

The earth hath bubbles, as the water has,
And these are of them.

Act i. Sc. 3.

Two truths are told,
As happy prologues to the swelling act
Of the imperial theme.

Act i. Sc. 3.

Present fears
Are less than horrible imaginings.

Act i. Sc. 3.

Come what come may,
Time and the hour runs through the roughest day.

Act i. Sc. 4.

Nothing in his life
Became him like the leaving it.

Act i. Sc. 4.

There's no art
To find the mind's construction in the face.

Act i. Sc. 5.

Yet I do fear thy nature;
It is too full of the milk of human kindness
To catch the nearest way.

Act i. Sc. 5.

Your face, my thane, is as a book, where men
May read strange matters.

Act i. Sc. 7.

If it were done, when 'tis done, then 'twere well
It were done quickly.

Act i. Sc. 7.

That but this blow
Might be the be-all and the end-all here.

Act i. Sc. 7.

This even-handed justice
Commends the ingredients of our poisoned chalice
To our own lips.

Act i. Sc. 7.

Besides, this Duncan
Hath borne his faculties so meek, hath been
So clear in his great office, that his virtues
Will plead like angels, trumpet-tongued, against
The deep damnation of his taking off.

Act i. Sc, 7.

I have no spur
To prick the sides of my intent, but only
Vaulting ambition, which o'erleaps itself,

And falls on the other--.

Act i. Sc. 7.

I have bought
Golden opinions from all sorts of people.

Act i. Sc. 7.

Letting *I dare not* wait upon *I would*.

Like the poor cat i' the adage.

Act i. Sc. 7.

I dare do all that may become a man;
Who dares do more, is none.

Act i. Sc. 7.

But screw your courage to the sticking-place.

Act ii. Sc. 1.

Is this a dagger which I see before me,
The handle towards my hand?

Act ii. Sc. 1.

Thou sure and firm-set earth,
Hear not my steps, which way they walk, for fear
The very stones prate of my whereabout.

Act ii. Sc. 1.

For it is a knell
That summons thee to heaven or to hell!

Act ii. Sc. 2.

The attempt, and not the deed,
Confound us.

Act ii. Sc. 2.

Sleep, that knits up the ravell'd sleave of care.

Act ii. Sc. 2.

Infirm of purpose!

Act ii. Sc. 3.

The labor we delight in, physics pain.

Act ii. Sc. 3.

The wine of life is drawn, and the mere lees
Is left this vault to brag of.

Act ii. Sc. 4.

A falcon, towering in her pride of place,
Was by a mousing owl hawked at, and killed.

Act iii. Sc, 1.

Upon my head they placed a fruitless crown,
And put a barren scepter in my gripe,
Thence to be wrenched with an unlineal hand,
No son of mine succeeding.

Act iii. Sc. 1.

Mur. We are men, my liege.
Mac. Ay, in the catalogue ye go for men.

Act iii. Sc. 2.

We have scotched the snake, not killed it.

Act iii. Sc. 2.

Duncan is in his grave!
After life's fitful fever he sleeps well.

Act iii. Sc. 4.

But now, I am cabined, cribbed, confined bound in
To saucy doubts and fears.

Act iii. Sc. 4.

Now good digestion wait on appetite,
And health on both!

Act iii. Sc. 4.

Thou canst not say, I did it: never shake
Thy gory locks at me.

Act iii. Sc. 4.

Thou hast no speculation in those eyes
Which thou dost glare with!

Act iii. Sc. 4.

What man dare, I dare.

Act iii. Sc. 4.

Take any shape but that, and my firm nerves
Shall never tremble.

Act iii. Sc. 4.

Stand not upon the order of your going,
But go at once.

Act iii. Sc. 4.

Can such things be,
And overcome us like a summer's cloud,
Without our special wonder?

Act iv. Sc. 1.

Black spirits and white,
Red spirits and gray,
Mingle, mingle, mingle,
You that mingle may.[2]

[Note 2: These lines occur also in "The Witch" of Thomas
Middleton, Act 5, Sc. 2, and it is uncertain to which the
priority should be ascribed.]

Act iv. Sc. 1.

By the pricking of my thumbs,
Something wicked this way comes.

Act iv. Sc. 1.

A deed without a name.

Act iv. Sc. 1.

I'll make assurance double sure,
And take a bond of fate.

Act iv. Sc. 1.

Show his eyes, and grieve his heart!
Come like shadows, so depart.

Act iv. Sc. 1.

What! will the line stretch out to the crack of doom?

Act iv. Sc. 1.
The flighty purpose never is o'ertook,
Unless the deed go with it.

Act iv. Sc. 3.

What, all my pretty chickens, and their dam,
At one fell swoop?

Act iv. Sc. 3.

I cannot but remember such things were,
That were most precious to me.

Act iv. Sc. 3.

O, I could play the woman with mine eyes,
And braggart with my tongue!

Act v. Sc. 3.

My way of life
Is fallen into the sear, the yellow leaf;
And that which should accompany old age,
As honor, love, obedience, troops of friends,
I must not look to have; but, in their stead,
Curses, not loud, but deep, mouth-honor, breath,
Which the poor heart would fain deny, but dare not.

Act v. Sc. 3.

Not so sick, my lord,
As she is troubled with thick-coming fancies,

That keep her from her rest.

Act v. Sc. 3.

Canst thou not minister to a mind diseased;
Pluck from the memory a rooted sorrow;
Raze out the written troubles of the brain;
And, with some sweet oblivious antidote,
Cleanse the stuffed bosom of that perilous stuff
Which weighs upon the heart?

Act v. Sc, 3.

Throw physic to the dogs: I'll none of it.

Act v. Sc. 3.

I would applaud thee to the very echo,
That should applaud again.

Act v, Sc. 5.

Hang out our banners on the outward walls;
The cry is still, *They come*.

Act v. Sc. 5.

To-morrow, and to-morrow, and to-morrow,

Creeps in this petty pace from day to day,
To the last syllable of recorded time;
And all our yesterdays have lighted fools
The way to dusty death. Out, out, brief candle!
Life's but a walking shadow; a poor player,
That struts and frets his hour upon the stage,
And then is heard no more; it is a tale
Told by an idiot, full of sound and fury,
Signifying nothing.

Act v. Sc. 5.

Blow, wind! come, wrack!
At least we'll die with harness on our back.

Act. v. Sc. 7.

I bear a charmed life.

Act. v. Sc. 7.

That keep the word of promise to our ear,
And break it to our hope.

Act v. Sc. 7.

Lay on, Macduff;
And damned be him that first cries, Hold, enough!

KING JOHN.

Act ii. Sc. 1.

For courage mounteth with occasion.

Act iii. Sc. 1.

Thou slave, thou wretch, thou coward,
Thou little valiant, great in villany!
Thou ever strong upon the stronger side!
Thou fortune's champion, that dost never fight
But when her humorous ladyship is by
To teach thee safety!

Thou wear a lion's hide! Doff it for shame,
And hang a calf's skin on those recreant limbs.

Act iii. Sc. 4.

Life is as tedious as a twice-told tale,
Vexing the dull ear of a drowsy man.

Act iv. Sc. 2.

To gild refined gold, to paint the lily,
To throw a perfume on the violet,

To smooth the ice, or add another hue
Unto the rainbow, or with taper-light
To seek the beauteous eye of heaven to garnish,
Is wasteful and ridiculous excess.

Act iv. Sc. 2.

Now oft the sight of means to do ill deeds
Makes deeds ill done!

KING RICHARD II.

Act i. Sc. 3.

Oh, who can hold a fire in his hand,
By thinking on the frosty Caucasus?
Or cloy the hungry edge of appetite,
By bare imagination of a feast?

Act i. Sc. 3.

The apprehension of the good
Gives but the greater feeling to the worse.

Act ii. Sc. 1.

The ripest fruit first falls.

FIRST PART OF KING HENRY IV.

Act i. Sc. 2.

'Tis my vocation, Hal; 'tis no sin for a man to labor in his vocation.

Act i. Sc. 2.

He will give the devil his due.

Act i. Sc. 3.

And, as the soldiers bore dead bodies by,
He called them untaught knaves, unmannerly,
To bring a slovenly, unhandsome corse
Betwixt the wind and his nobility.

Act i. Sc. 3.

By heaven, methinks it were an easy leap,
To pluck bright honor from the pale-faced moon.

Act ii. Sc. 1.

I know a trick worth two of that.

Act ii. Sc. 4.

Call you that backing of your friends? a plague upon such backing!

Act ii. Sc. 4.

A plague of sighing and grief! it blows a man up like a bladder.

Act ii. Sc. 4.

Give you a reason on compulsion! if reasons were as plenty as blackberries, I would give no man a reason upon compulsion.

Act ii. Sc. 4.

I was a coward on instinct.

Act ii. Sc. 4.

No more of that, Hal, an thou lovest me.

Act iii. Sc. 1.

Glen. I can call spirits from the vasty deep.
Hot. Why, so can I, or so can any man: But will they come when you do call for them?

Act iii. Sc. 1.

Tell truth and shame the devil.

Act iii. Sc. 1.

I had rather be a kitten, and cry mew,
Than one of these same meter ballad-mongers.

Act iii. Sc. 3.

Shall I not take mine ease in mine inn?

Act v. Sc. 4.

I could have better spared a better man.

Act v. Sc. 4.

The better part of valor is--discretion.

Act v. Sc. 4.

Lord, Lord, how this world is given to lying! I grant you, I was down, and out of breath; and so was he: but we rose both at an instant, and fought a long hour by Shrewsbury clock.

SECOND PART OF KING HENRY IV.

Act i. Sc. 1.

Even such a man, so faint, so spiritless.
So dull, so dead in look, so woebegone,
Drew Priam's curtain in the dead of night,
And would have told him, half his Troy was burned.

Act i. Sc. 1.

Yet the first bringer of unwelcome news
Hath but a losing office; and his tongue
Sounds ever after as a sullen bell,
Remembered knolling a departed friend.

Act i. Sc. 2.

I am not only witty in myself, but the cause that wit is in other men.

Act ii. Sc. 2.

He hath eaten me out of house and home.

Act ii. Sc. 3.

He was, indeed, the glass

Wherein the noble youth did dress themselves.

Act iii. Sc. 1.

Sleep, gentle sleep,
Nature's soft nurse, how have I frighted thee,
That thou no more wilt weigh my eyelids down,
And steep my senses in forgetfulness?

Act iii. Sc. 1.

With all appliances and means to boot.

Act iii. Sc. 1.

Uneasy lies the head that wears a crown.

Act iv. Sc. 4.

He hath a tear for pity, and a hand
Open as day for melting charity.

Act iv. Sc. 4.

Thy wish was father, Harry, to that thought.

Act v. Sc. 3.

Under which king, Bezonian? Speak, or die.

KING HENRY V.

Act i. Sc. 1.

Consideration like an angel came,
And whipped the offending Adam out of him.

Act i, Sc. 1.

When he speaks,
The air, a chartered libertine, is still.

Act ii Sc. 1.

Base is the slave that pays.

Act ii. Sc. 3.

'A babbled of green fields.

Act iv. Chorus.

With busy hammers closing rivets up,
Give dreadful note of preparation.

Act iv. Sc. 3.

Then shall our names,
Familiar in their mouths as household words--
Harry the King, Bedford and Exeter,
Warwick and Talbot, Salisbury and Gloster--
Be in their flowing cups freshly remembered.

FIRST PART OF KING HENRY VI.

Act v. Sc. 3.

She's beautiful; and therefore to be wooed:
She is a woman; therefore to be won.

SECOND PART OF KING HENRY VI.

Act iii. Sc. 1.

Smooth runs the water where the brook is deep.

Act iii. Sc. 2.

What stronger breastplate than a heart untainted?
Thrice is he armed that hath his quarrel just;
And he but naked, though locked up in steel,
Whose conscience with injustice is corrupted.

Act iii. Sc. 3.

He dies and makes no sign.

THIRD PART OF KING HENRY VI.

Act v. Sc. 6.

Suspicion always haunts the guilty mind;
The thief doth fear each bush an officer.

KING RICHARD III

Act i. Sc. 1.

Now is the winter of our discontent
Made glorious summer by this sun of York;
And all the clouds that lowered upon our house,
In the deep bosom of the ocean buried.

Act i. Sc. 1.

Cheated of feature by dissembling nature,
Deformed, unfinished, Bent before my time
Into this breathing world, scarce half made up.

Act i. Sc. 1.

Why I, in this weak, piping time of peace,
Have no delight to pass away the time.

Act i. Sc. 2.

To leave this keen encounter of our wits.

Act i. Sc. 2.

Was ever woman in this humor wooed?
Was ever woman in this humor won?

Act i. Sc. 4.

O, I have passed a miserable night,
So full of fearful dreams, of ugly sights,
That, as I am a Christian faithful man,
I would not spend another such a night,
Though 'twere to buy a world of happy days.

Act iv. Sc. 2.

Thou troublest me; I am not in the vein.

Act iv. Sc. 4.

Let not the heavens hear these telltale women
Hail on the Lord's anointed.

Act iv. Sc. 4.

An honest tale speeds best, being plainly told

Act v. Sc. 2.

Thus far into the bowels of the land
Have we marched on without impediment.

Act v. Sc. 2.

True hope is swift, and flies with swallow's wings,
Kings it makes gods, and meaner creatures kings.

Act v. Sc. 3.

The king's name is a tower of strength.

Act v. Sc. 4.

I have set my life upon a cast,
And I will stand the hazard of the die.

Act v. Sc. 4.

A horse! a horse! My kingdom for a horse!

KING HENRY VIII.

Act ii. Sc. 3.

Verily,
I swear, 'tis better to be lowly born,
And range with humble livers in content,
Than to be perked up in a glistering grief,
And wear a golden sorrow.

Act iii. Sc. 2.

And then to breakfast with
What appetite you have.

Act iii. Sc. 2.

Farewell, a long farewell, to all my greatness!
This is the state of man. To-day he puts forth
The tender leaves of hopes; to-morrow blossoms
And bears his blushing honors thick upon him.

Act iii. Sc. 2.

O how wretched
Is that poor man that hangs on princes' favors!
There is, betwixt that smile we would aspire to
That sweet aspect of princes, and their ruin,
More pangs and fears than wars or women have;
And when he falls, he falls like Lucifer,
Never to hope again.

Act iii. Sc. 2.

Had I but served my God with half the zeal
I served my king, he would not in mine age
Have left me naked to mine enemies.

Act iv. Sc. 2.

Men's evil manners live in brass; their virtues
We write in water.

Act v. Sc. 2.

To dance attendance on their lordship's pleasures.

TROILUS AND CRESSIDA.

Act iii. Sc. 3.

One touch of nature makes the whole world kin

Act iii. Sc. 3.

And, like a dewdrop from the lion's mane,
Be shook to air.

CORIOLANUS.

Act iii. Sc. 1.

Hear you this Triton of the minnows?

JULIUS CAESAR.

Act i. Sc. 2.

Beware the Ides of March!

Act i. Sc. 2.

I cannot tell what you and other men
Think of this life; but for my single self,
I had as lief not be as live to be
In awe of such a thing as I myself.

Act i. Sc. 2.

Dar'st thou, Cassius, now
Leap in with me into this angry flood,
And swim to yonder point?--Upon the word,
Accoutred as I was, I plunged in,
And bade him follow.

Act i. Sc. 2.

Ye gods, it doth amaze me,
A man of such a feeble temper should
So get the start of the majestic world,
And bear the palm alone.

Act i. Sc. 2.

Why, man, he doth bestride the narrow world,
Like a Colossus, and we petty men
Walk under his huge legs, and peep about
To find ourselves dishonorable graves.

Act i. Sc. 2.

Let me have men about me that are fat;
Sleek-headed men, and such as sleep o' nights;
Yond' Cassius has a lean and hungry look;
He thinks too much: such men are dangerous.

Act i. Sc. 2.

Seldom he smiles; and smiles in such a sort,
As if he mocked himself, and scorned his spirit,
That could be moved to smile at anything.

Act i. Sc. 2.

But, for mine own part, it was Greek to me.

Act ii. Sc. 1.

Between the acting of a dreadful thing
And the first motion, all the interim is
Like a phantasma, or a hideous dream.

Act ii. Sc. 1.

Yon are my true and honorable wife,
As dear to me as the ruddy drops
That visit my sad heart.

Act ii. Sc. 2.

Cowards die many times before their deaths;
The valiant never taste of death but once.

Act iii. Sc. 1.

Though last, not least, in love.

Act iii. Sc. 1.

Cry **Havoc**, and let slip the dogs of war.

Act iii. Sc. 2.

Romans, countrymen, and lovers! hear me
for my cause; and be silent that you may hear.

Act iii. Sc. 2.

Not that I loved Caesar less, but that I loved
Rome more.

Act iii. Sc. 2.

Who is here so base, that would be a bondman?
If any, speak: for him have I offended.

Act iii. Sc. 2..

The evil that men do lives after them;
The good is oft interred with their bones.

Act iii. Sc. 2.

For Brutus is an honorable man;
So are they all, all honorable men.

Act iii. Sc. 2.

When that the poor have cried, Caesar hath wept;
Ambition should be made of sterner stuff.

Act iii. Sc. 2.

But yesterday, the word of Caesar might
Have stood against the world; now lies he there,
And none so poor to do him reverence.

Act iii. Sc. 2.

If you have years, prepare to shed them now.

Act iii. Sc. 2.

See, what a rent the envious Casca made!

Act iii. Sc. 2.

This was the most unkindest cut of all.

Act iii. Sc. 2.

Great Caesar fell.
O what a fall was there, my countrymen!

Act iii. Sc. 2.

Put a tongue
In every wound of Caesar, that should move
The stones of Borne to rise and mutiny.

Act iv. Sc. 2.

There are no tricks in plain and simple faith.

Act iv. Sc. 3.

I had rather be a dog, and bay the moon,
Than such a Roman.

Act iv. Sc. 3.

There is no terror, Cassius, in your threats
For I am armed so strong in honesty,

That they pass by me as the idle wind,
Which I respect not.

Act iv. Sc. 3.

A friend should bear a friend's infirmities,
But Brutus makes mine greater than they are.

Act iv. Sc. 3.

There is a tide in the affairs of men,
Which, taken at the flood, leads on to fortune:
Omitted, all the voyage of their life
Is bound in shallows, and in miseries.

Act v. Sc. 5.

His life was gentle, and the elements
So mixed in him, that nature might stand up
And say to all the world, *This was a man*!

ANTONY AND CLEOPATRA.

Act i. Sc. 1.

There's beggary in the love that can be reckoned.

Act ii. Sc. 2.

For her own person,
It beggared all description.

Act ii. Sc. 2.

Age cannot wither her, nor custom stale
Her infinite variety.

CYMBELINE.

Act ii. Sc. 3.

Hark! hark! the lark at heaven's gate sings,

Act iii. Sc. 2.

Some griefs are med'cinable.

Act iii. Sc. 6.

Weariness
Can snore upon the flint, when restive sloth
Finds the down pillow hard.

KING LEAR.

Act i. Sc. 4.

How sharper than a serpent's tooth it is,
To have a thankless child.

Act i. Sc. 4.

Striving to better, oft we mar what's well.

Act ii. Sc. 4.

O, let not women's weapons, water-drops,
Stain my man's cheeks.

Act iil. Sc. 2.

Blow, wind, and crack your cheeks! rage! blow!

Act iii. Sc. 2.

Tremble, thou wretch,
That hast within thee undivulged crimes,
Unwhipped of justice.

Act iii. Sc. 2.

I am a man
More sinned against than sinning.

Act iii. Sc. 4.

Poor naked wretches, wheresoe'er you are,
That bide the pelting of this pitiless storm,
How shall your houseless heads, and unfed sides,
Your looped and windowed raggedness, defend you
From seasons such as these?
Take physic, pomp;
Expose thyself to feel what wretches feel.

Act iii. Sc. 4.

I'll talk a word with this same learned Theban.

Act iii. Sc. 6.

The little dogs and all,
Tray, Blanch, and Sweetheart, see, they bark at me.

Act iv. Sc. 6.

Ay, every inch a king.

Act. iv. Sc. 6.

Give me an ounce of civet, good apothecary,
to sweeten my imagination.

Act iv. Sc. 6.

Through tattered clothes small vices do appear;
Robes and furred gowns hide all.

Act v. Sc. 3.

The gods are just, and of our pleasant vices
Make instruments to plague us.

Act. v. Sc. 3.

Her voice was ever soft,
Gentle, and low; an excellent thing in woman.

ROMEO AND JULIET.

Act i. Sc. 1.

The weakest goes to the wall.

Act i. Sc. 2.

One fire burns out another's burning.
One pain is lessened by another's anguish.

Act i. Sc. 5.

Too early seen unknown, and known too late,

Act ii. Sc. 2.

He jests at scars, that never felt a wound.

Act ii. Sc. 2.

See, how she leans her cheek upon her hand!
O that I were a glove upon that hand,
That I might touch that cheek!

Act ii. Sc. 2.

O Romeo, Romeo! wherefore art thou Romeo?

Act ii. Sc. 2.

What's in a name? that which we call a rose
By any other name would smell as sweet.

Act ii. Sc. 2.

Alack! there lies more peril in thine eye,
Than twenty of their swords.

Act ii. Sc. 2.

At lover's perjuries,
They say, Jove laughs.

Act ii. Sc. 2.

O swear not by the moon, the inconstant moon,
That monthly changes in her circled orb,
Lest that thy love prove likewise variable.

Act ii. Sc. 2.

Good-night, good-night! parting is such sweet sorrow,
That I shall say good-night till it be morrow.

Act ii. Sc. 3.

Thy old groans ring yet in my ancient ears

Act ii. Sc. 4.

Stabbed with a white wench's black eye.

Act ii. Sc. 4.

I am the very pink of courtesy.

Act ii. Sc. 4.

My man's as true as steel.

Act ii, Sc. 6.

Here comes the lady;--O, so light a foot
Will ne'er wear out the everlasting flint.

Act iii. Sc, 1.

A plague o' both the houses!

Act iii. Sc. 1.

Rom. Courage, man I the hurt cannot be much.
Mer. No, 'tis not so deep as a well, nor so wide as a church-door;
but 'tis enough.

Act iii. Sc. 3.

Adversity's sweet milk, philosophy

Act iii. Sc. 5.

Night's candles are burnt out, and jocund day
Stands tiptoe on the misty mountain-tops.

Act iv. Sc. 2.

Not stopping o'er the bounds of modesty.

Act v. Sc. I.

My bosom's lord sits lightly in his throne.

Act v. Sc. 1.

A beggarly account of empty boxes.

Act v. Sc. 1.

My poverty, but not my will, consents.

Act v. Sc. 3.

Beauty's ensign yet
Is crimson in thy lips, and in thy cheeks,
And death's pale flag is not advanced there.

Act v. Sc. 3.

Eyes, look your last!
Arms, take your last embrace!

HAMLET.

Act i. Sc. 1.

This bodes some strange eruption to our state.

Act i. Sc. 1.

In the most high and palmy state of Rome,
A little ere the mightiest Julius fell,
The graves stood tenantless, and the sheeted dead
Did squeak and gibber in the Roman streets.

Act i. Sc. 1.

And then it started like a guilty thing
Upon a fearful summons.

Act i. Sc. 1.

Some say, that ever 'gainst that season comes
Wherein our Saviour's birth is celebrated,
This bird of dawning singeth all night long.
And then they say no spirit dares stir abroad,

The nights are wholesome; then no planets strike,
No fairy takes, nor witch hath power to charm,
So hallowed and so gracious is the time.

Act i. Sc. 2.

The head is not more native to the heart.

Act i. Sc. 2.

A little more than kin, and less than kind.

Act i, Sc. 2.

Seems, madam! nay, it is; I know not seems

Act i. Sc. 2.

But I have that within which passeth show;
These, but the trappings and the suits of woe.

Act i. Sc. 2.

O that this too, too solid flesh would melt,
Thaw, and resolve itself into a dew!
Or that the Everlasting had not fixed
His canon 'gainst self-slaughter! O God! O God!
How weary, stale, flat, and unprofitable

Seem to me all the uses of this world!
That it should come to this!
Hyperion to a satyr! so loving to my mother,
That he might not beteem the winds of heaven
Visit her face too roughly.
Why, she would hang on him,
As if increase of appetite had grown
By what it fed on.
Frailty, thy name is woman!
A little month.
Like Niobe, all tears.
My father's brother; but no more like my father
Than I to Hercules.

Act i. Sc. 2.

Thrift, thrift, Horatio! the funeral baked meats
Did coldly furnish forth the marriage tables.

Act i. Sc. 2.

In my mind's eye, Horatio.

Act i. Sc. 2.

He was a man, take him for all in all,
I shall not look upon his like again.

Act i. Sc. 2.

A countenance more
In sorrow than in anger.

Act i. Sc. 3.

And in the morn and liquid dew of youth.

Act i. Sc. 3.

Be thou familiar, but by no means vulgar.
The friends thou hast, and their adoption tried
Grapple them to thy soul with hooks of steel.
Give every man thy ear, but few thy voice.
Costly thy habit as thy purse can buy,
But not expressed in fancy; rich, not gaudy;
For the apparel oft proclaims the man.
Neither a borrower nor a lender be.

Act i. Sc. 3.

Springes to catch woodcocks.

Act i. Sc. 4.

But to my mind--though I am native here,
And to the manner born--it is a custom
More honored in the breach than the observance.

Act i. Sc. 4.

Angels and ministers of grace, defend us!

Act i. Sc. 4.

Thou com'st in such a questionable shape,
That I will speak to thee.

Act i. Sc. 4.

Let me not burst in ignorance!

Act i. Sc. 4.

I do not set my life at a pin's fee.

Act i. Sc. 4.

Something is rotten in the state of Denmark.

Act i. Sc. 5.

I could a tale unfold, whose lightest word
Would harrow up thy soul; freeze thy young blood;
Make thy two eyes, like stars, start from their spheres;
Thy knotted and combined locks to part,
And each particular hair to stand on end,

Like quills upon the fretful Porcupine.

Act i. Sc. 5.

O my prophetic soul! my uncle!

Act i. Sc. 5.

O Hamlet, what a falling-off was there!

Act i. Sc. 5.

No reckoning made, but sent to my account
With all my imperfections on my head.

Act i. Sc. 5.

The glowworm shows the matin to be near
And 'gins to pale his uneffectual fire.

Act i. Sc. 5.

There needs no ghost, my lord, come from the grave,
To tell us this.

Act i. Sc. 5.

There are more things in heaven and earth, Horatio,
Than are dreamt of in your philosophy.

Act i. Sc. 5.

The time is out of joint.

Act ii. Sc. 1.

This is the very ecstasy of love.

Act ii. Sc. 2.

Brevity is the soul of wit.

Act ii. Sc. 2.

That he is mad, 'tis true; 'tis true, 'tis pity;
And pity 'tis, 'tis true.

Act ii. Sc. 2.

Doubt thou the stars are tire;
Doubt that the sun doth move;
Doubt truth to be a liar;
But never doubt I love.

Act ii. Sc. 2,

Still harping on my daughter.

Act ii. Sc. 2.

Though this be madness, yet there's method in it.

Act ii. Sc. 2.

What a piece of work is man! How noble in reason! how infinite in faculties! in form and moving, how express and admirable! in action, how like an angel! in apprehension, how like a God!

Act ii. Sc. 2.

Man delights not me--nor woman neither.

Act ii. Sc. 2.

I know a hawk from a hand-saw.

Act ii. Sc. 2.

Come, give us a taste of your quality.

Act ii. Sc. 2.

'Twas caviare to the general.

Act ii. Sc. 2.

What's Hecuba to him, or he to Hecuba?

Act ii. Sc. 2.

The play's the thing,
Wherein I'll catch the conscience of the king.

Act iii. Sc. 1.

To be, or not to be? that is the question:
Whether 'tis nobler in the mind, to suffer
The slings and arrows of outrageous fortune,
Or to take arms against a sea of troubles,
And, by opposing, end them?--To die--to sleep--
No more--and, by a sleep, to say we end
The heartache, and the thousand natural shocks
That flesh is heir to--'tis a consummation
Devoutly to be wished. To die--to sleep--
To sleep! perchance, to dream--ay, there's the rub;
For in that sleep of death what dreams may come,
When we have shuffled off this mortal coil,
Must give us pause.
The spurns
That patient merit of the unworthy takes;

When he himself might his quietus make
With a bare bodkin. Who would fardels bear,
To grunt and sweat under a weary life,
But that the dread of something after death--
The undiscovered country, from whose bourne
No traveler returns--puzzles the will,
And makes us rather bear those ills we have,
Than fly to others that we know not of?
Thus conscience does make cowards of us all,
And thus the native hue of resolution
Is sicklied o'er with the pale cast of thought.
Nymph, in thy orisons
Be all my sins remembered.

Act iii. Sc. 1.

Be thou as chaste as ice, as pure as snow,
thon shalt not escape calumny.

Act iii. Sc. 1.

The glass of fashion, and the mould of form,
The observed of all observers!

Act iii. Sc. X.

Now see that noble and most sovereign reason,
Like sweet bells jangled, out of tune and harsh.

Act iii. Sc. 2.

It out-herods Herod.

Act iii. Sc. 2.

Suit the action to the word, the word to the action.

Act iii. Sc. 2.

To hold, as 'twere, the mirror up to nature.

Act iii. Sc. 2.

I have thought some of nature's journeymen had made men, and not made them well, they imitated humanity so abominably.

Act iii. Sc. 2.

No, let the candied tongue lick absurd pomp;
And crook the pregnant hinges of the knee,
Where thrift may follow fawning.

Act iii. Sc. 2.

Give me that man
That is not passion's slave, and I will wear him
In my heart's core, ay, in my heart of hearts,

As I do thee.

Act iii. Sc. 2.

Something too much of this.

Act iii. Sc. 2.

Here's metal more attractive.

Act iii. Sc. 2.

The lady doth protest too much, methinks.

Act iii. Sc. 2.

Let the galled jade wince, our withers are un-wrung.

Act iii. Sc. 2.

Why, let the strucken deer go weep,
The hart ungalled play;
For some must watch, while some must sleep;
Thus runs the world away.

Act iii. Sc. 2.

It will discourse most eloquent music.

Act iii. Sc. 2.

Very like a whale.

Act iii. Sc. 2.

They fool me to the top of my bent.

Act iii. Sc. 2.

'Tis now the very witching time of night,
When churchyards yawn, and hell itself breathes out
Contagion to this world.

Act iii. Sc. 3.

O my offence is rank, it smells to heaven

Act iii. Sc. 4.

Look here, upon this picture, and on this;
The counterfeit presentment of two brothers.
See what a grace was seated on this brow!
Hyperion's curls; the front of Jove himself;

An eye like Mars, to threaten and command.
A combination, and a form, indeed,
Where every god did seem to set his seal,
To give the world assurance of a man.

Act iii. Sc. 4.

A king Of shreds and patches.

Act iii. Sc. 4.

This is the very coinage of your brain.

Act iii. Sc. 4.

Lay not that flattering unction to your soul.

Act iii. Sc. 4.

Assume a virtue, if you have it not.

Act iii. Sc. 4.

For 'tis the sport to have the engineer
Hoist with his own petard.

Act iv. Sc. **5.**

When sorrows come, they come not single spies,
But in battalions!

Act iv. Sc. **5.**

There's such divinity doth hedge a king,
That treason can but peep to what it would.

Act v. Sc. 1.

How absolute the knave is! we must speak by the card, or equivocation
will undo us.

Act v. Sc. 1.

Alas, poor Yorick! I knew him, Horatio: a fellow of infinite jest; of
most excellent fancy.

Act v. Sc. 1.

Where be your gibes now? your gambols? your songs? your flashes of
merriment, that were wont to set the table on a roar?

Act v. Sc. 1.

To what base uses we may return, Horatio!

Act v. Sc. 1.

Imperial Caesar, dead, and turned to clay, Might stop a hole to keep the wind away.

Act v. Sc. 1.

Sir, though I am not splenetive and rash, Yet have I in me something dangerous.

Act v. Sc. 1.

The cat will mew, and dog will have his day.

Act v. Sc. 2.

There's a divinity that shapes our ends, Rough-hew them how we will.

Act v. Sc. 2.

There is a special providence in the fall of a sparrow.

Act v. Sc. 2.

A hit, a very palpable hit.

OTHELLO.

Act i. Sc. 1.

But I will wear my heart upon my sleeve
For daws to peck at.

Act i. Sc. 3.

Most potent, grave, and reverend seigniors.

Act i. Sc. 3.

The very head and front of my offending
Hath this extent, no more.

Act i. Sc. 3.

I will a round, unvarnished tale deliver
Of my whole course of love.

Act i. Sc. 3.

Wherein I spoke of most disastrous chances,
Of moving accidents, by flood and field;
Of hair-breadth 'scapes i' the imminent deadly breach.

Act i. Sc. 3.

My story being done
She gave me for my pains a world of signs:
She swore, In faith, 'twas strange, 'twas passing; strange;
'Twas pitiful, 'twas wondrous pitiful:
She wished she had not heard it; yet she
wished
That Heaven had made her such a man.

Act i. Sc. 3.

Upon this hint I spake.

Act i. Sc. 3.

I do perceive hero a divided duty.

Act ii. Sc. 1.

For I am nothing, if not critical.

Act ii. Sc. 1.

Iago. To suckle fools, and chronicle small beer.

Des. O most lame and impotent conclusion!

Act ii. Sc. 3.

Silence that dreadful bell; it frights the isle
From her propriety.

Act ii. Sc. 3.

O thou invisible spirit of wine, if thou hast
no name to be known by, let us call thee devil!

Act ii. Sc. 3.

O that men should put an enemy in their
mouths, to steal away their brains!

Act iii. Sc. 3.

Perdition catch my soul,
But I do love thee! and when I love thee not,
Chaos is come again.

Act iii. Sc. 3.

Good name, in man and woman, dear my lord,
Is the immediate jewel of their souls.
Who steals my purse, steals trash; 'tis something, nothing;
'Twas mine, 'tis his, and has been slave to thousands;
But he that filches from me my good name
Robs roe of that which not enriches him,

And makes me poor indeed.

Act iii. Sc. 3.

O, beware, my lord, of jealousy;
It is the green-eyed monster, which doth make
The meat it feeds on.

Act iii. Sc. 3.

Trifles, light as air,
Are, to the jealous, confirmations strong
As proofs of holy writ.

Act iii. Sc. 3.

Not poppy, nor mandragora,
Nor all the drowsy sirups of the world,
Shall ever medicine thee to that sweet sleep
Which thou ow'dst yesterday.

Act iii. Sc. 3.

He that is robbed, not wanting what is stolen,
Let him not know it, and he's not robbed at all.

Act iii. Sc. 3.

O, now, forever,
Farewell the tranquil mind! farewell content!
Farewell the plumed troop, and the big wars,
That make ambition virtue! O farewell!
Farewell the neighing steed, and the shrill trump,
The spirit-stirring drum, the ear-piercing fife,
Othello's occupation's gone!

Act iii. Sc. 3.

Give me the ocular proof.

Act iii. Sc. 3.

But this denoted a foregone conclusion.

Act iv. Sc. 1.

They laugh that win.

Act iv. Sc. 2.

Steeped me in poverty to the very lips.

Act iv. Sc. 2.

But, alas! to make me
A fixed figure, for the time of scorn
To point his slow, unmovin finger at.

Act iv. Sc. 2.

And put in every honest hand a whip,
To lash the rascal naked through the world.

Act iv. Sc. 3.

'Tis neither here nor there.

Act v. Sc. 1.

He hath a daily beauty in his life.

Act v. Sc. 2.

I have done the state some service, and they know it.

Act v. Sc. 2.

Speak of me as I am; nothing extenuate,
Nor set down aught in malice.
Then must you speak.
Of one that loved not wisely, but too well.

Of one, whose hand,
Like the base Judean, threw a pearl away,
Richer than all his tribe.
Albeit unused to the melting mood.

THOMAS TUSSER.
1523-1580.

Moral Reflections on the Wind.

Except wind stands as never it stood,
It is an ill wind turns none to good.

FULKE GREVILLE, LORD BROOKE.
1554-1624.

Mustapha. Act v. Sc. 4.

O wearisome condition of humanity!

Sonnet LVI.

And out of minde as soon as out of sight.

CHRISTOPHER MARLOWE.
1565-1593.

Hero and Leander.

Who ever loved that loved not at first sight.

The Passionate Shepherd to his Love.

Come live with me, and be my love,
And we will all the pleasures prove
That valleys, groves, and hills, and folds,
Woods, or steepy mountains, yield.

SIR WALTER RALEIGH.
1552-1618.

The Nymph's Reply to the Passionate Shepherd.

If all the world and love were young,
And truth in every shepherd's tongue,
These pretty pleasures might me move
To live with thee, and be thy love.

The Silent Lover.

Silence in love betrays more love
Than words, though ne'er so witty;
A beggar that is dumb, you know,
May challenge double pity.

JOSHUA SYLVESTER
1563-1618.

The Soul's Errand[3]

Go, Soul, the body's guest,
Upon a thankless errand!
Fear not to touch the best:
The truth shall be thy warrant.
Go, since I needs must die,
And give the world the lie.

[Note 3: Sylvester is now generally regarded as the author of
"The Soul's Errand," long attributed to Raleigh.]

RICHARD BARNFIELD.

Address to the Nightingale.[4]

As it fell upon a day,
In the merry mouth of May,
Sitting in a pleasant shade
Which a grove of myrtles made.

[Note 4: This song, often attributed to Shakespeare, is now confidently
assigned to Barnfield, and it is found in his collection
of Poems, published between 1594 and 1598.]

EDMUND SPENSER.
1553-1597.

Faerie Queene.

Book i. Canto i. St. 35.

The noblest mind the best contentment has.

Book 1. Canto iii. St. 4.

Her angels face,
As the great eye of heaven, shyned bright,
And made a sunshine in the shady place.

Book i. Canto ix. St. 35.

That darkesome cave they enter, where they find
That cursed man, low sitting on the ground,
Musing full sadly in his sullein mind.

Book ii. Canto vi. St. 12.

No daintie flowre or herbe that growes on grownd
No arborett with painted blossomes drest
And smelling sweete, but there it might be fownd
To bud out faire, and throwe her sweete smels al arownd.

Book iv. Canto ii. St.

Dan Chaucer, well of English undefyled.

Lines on his Promised Pension.

I was promised on a time
To have reason for my rhyme;
From that time unto this season,
I received nor rhyme nor reason.

Hymn in Honor of Beauty. Line 132.

For of the soul the body form doth take,
For soul is form, and doth the Body make.

MOTHER HUBBERD'S TALE.

Full little knowest thou that hast not tride,
What hell it is in suing long to bide;
To loose good dayes, that might be better spent
To wast long nights in pensive discontent;
To speed to-day, to be put back to-morrow;
To feed on hope, to pine with feare and sorrow;
To fret thy soule with crosses and with cares;
To eate thy heart through comfortlesse dispaires;
To fawne, to crowche, to waite, to ride, to ronne,
To spend, to give, to want, to be undonne.

SIR HENRY WOTTON.
1568-1639.

The Character of a Happy Life.

How happy is he born and taught,
That serveth not another's will;
Whose armor is his honest thought,
And simple truth his utmost skill!
Lord of himself, though not of lands;

And having nothing, yet hath all.

To his Mistress, the Queen of Bohemia.

You meaner beauties of the night,
That poorly satisfy our eyes
More by your number than your light!

DR. JOHN DONNE.
1573-1631.

FUNERAL ELEGIES, ON THE PROGRESS OF THE SOUL.

The Second Anniversary. Line 245.

We understood
Her by her sight; her pure and eloquent blood
Spoke in her cheeks, and so distinctly wrought,
That one might almost say her body thought.

Elegy 8. *The Comparison*.

She and comparisons are odious.

BEN JONSON.
1571-1637.

To Celia.

(From "The Forest.")
Drink to me only with thine eyes,
And I will pledge with mine;
Or leave a kiss but in the cup,
And I'll not look for wine.

The Sweet Neglect. (From the "Silent Woman." Act i. Sc. 5.)

Still to be neat, still to be drest
As you were going to a feast.
Give me a look, give me a face,
That makes simplicity a grace.

Good Life, *Long Life*.

In small proportion we just beauties see,
And in short measures life may perfect be.

Epitaph on Elizabeth.

Underneath this stone doth lie
As much beauty as could die;
Which in life did harbor give
To more virtue than doth live.

Epitaph on the Countess of Pembroke.

Underneath this sable hearse
Lies the subject of all verse,
Sidney's sister, Pembroke's mother.
Death! ere thou hast slain another,
Learned and fair and good as she,
Time shall throw a dart at thee.

To the Memory of Shakespeare.

Soul of the age!
The applause! delight! the wonder of our stage!
My Shakespeare rise.
Small Latin, and less Greek.
He was not of an age, but for all time.
Sweet swan of Avon!

Every Man in his Humor. Act. ii. Sc. 3.

Get money; still get money, boy;
No matter by what means.

FRANCIS BEAUMONT.
1585-1616.

Letter to Ben Jonson.

What things have we seen
Done at the Mermaid! heard words that have been
So nimble, and so full of subtile flame,
As if that every one from whence they came
Had meant to put his whole wit in a jest,
And resolved to live a fool the rest
Of his dull life.

GEORGE WITHER.
1588-1667.

The Shepherd's Resolution.

Shall I, wasting in despair,
Dye because a woman's fair?
Or make pale my cheeks with care,
'Cause another's rosie are?
If she be not so to me,
What care I how faire she be?

FRANCIS QUARLES.
1592-1644.

Emblems. Book ii. 2.

Be wisely worldly, be not worldly wise.

Book ii. Epigram 10.

This house is to be let for life or years;
Her rent is sorrow, and her income tears,
Cupid 't has long stood void; her bills make known,
She must be dearly let, or let alone.

GEORGE HERBERT.
1593-1632.

Virtue.

Sweet day, so cool, so cairn, so bright,
The bridall of the earth and skies.
Only a sweet and virtuous soul,
Like seasoned timber, never gives.
SIR JOHN SUCKLING.
1608-1644.

On a Wedding.

Her feet beneath her petticoat,
Like little mice, stole in and out,
As if they feared the light;
But oh! she dances such a way!
No sun upon an Easter-day
Is half so fine a sight.
Her lips were red, and one was thin,
Compared with that was next her chin,
Some bee had stung it newly.

Song.

Why so pale and wan, fond lover,
Prithee, why so pale?
Will, when looking well can't move her,
Looking ill prevail?
Prithee, why so pale?

ROBERT HERRICK.
1591-1660.

The Rock of Rubies, and the Quarrie of Pearls.

Some asked me where the Rubies grew,
And nothing I did say;
But with my finger pointed to
The lips of Julia.
Some asked how Pearls did grow, and where?
Then spoke I to my Girl,
To part her lips, and showed them there
The quarelets of Pearl.

On her Feet.

Her pretty feet, like snails, did creep
A little out, and then,
As if they played at Bo-peep,
Did soon draw in again.

To the Virgins to make much of Time.

Gather ye rosebuds while ye may,
Old Time is still a-flying,
And this same flower, that smiles to-day,
To-morrow will be dying.

Night Piece to Julia.

Her eyes the glowworm lend thee,
The shooting stars attend thee;
And the elves also,
Whose little eyes glow
Like the sparks of fire, befriend thee.

SIR RICHARD LOVELACE.
1618-1658.

Orpheus to Beasts.

Oh! could you view the melody
Of every grace,
And music of her face,
You'd drop a tear;
Seeing more harmony
In her bright eye,
Than now you hear.

To Lucasta on Going to the Wars.

I could not love thee, dear, so much,
Loved I not honor more.

To Althea from Prison.

Stone walls do not a prison make,
Nor iron barres a cage;

Mindes innocent, and quiet, take
That for an hermitage.

JAMES SHIRLEY.
1596-1666.

Contention of Ajax and Ulysses.

Only the actions of the just
Smell sweet and blossom in the dust.

RICHARD CRASHAW.
--1650.

The conscious water saw its God and blushed.[5]

[Note 5: Lympha pudica Deum vidit et erubuit.--Latin Poems]

In Praise of Lessius' Rule of Health.

A happy soul, that all the way
To heaven hath a summer's day.

THOMAS DEKKER.
--1638.

Old Fortunatus.

And though mine arm should conquer twenty worlds,
There's a lean fellow beats all conquerors.

Honest Whore. P. ii. Act i. Sc. 2.

We are ne'er like angels till our passion dies.

ABRAHAM COWLEY.
1618-1667.

The Waiting-Maid.

Th' adorning thee with so much art
Is but a barb'rous skill;
'Tis like the poisoning of a dart,
Too apt before to kill.

The Motto.

What shall I do to be forever known,

And make the age to come my own?

On the Death of Crashaw.

His *faith*, perhaps, in some nice tenets might
Be wrong; his *life*, I'm sure, was in the right.

The Garden. Essay V.

God the first garden made, and the first city Cain.

SIR JOHN DENHAM.
1615-1679.

Cooper's Hill.

O could I flow like thee, and make thy stream
My great example, as it is my theme!

Though deep, yet clear; though gentle, yet not dull;
Strong without rage; without o'erflowing, full.

The Sophy. *A Tragedy*.

Actions of the last age are like Almanacs of the last year.

THOMAS CAREW.
1589-1639.

Disdain Returned.

He that loves a rosy cheek,
Or a coral lip admires,
Or from star-like eyes doth seek
Fuel to maintain his fires;
As old Time makes these decay,
So his flames must waste away.

Conquest by Flight.

Then fly betimes, for only they
Conquer love, that run away.

EDMUND WALLER.
1605-1687.

Verses upon his Divine Poesy.

The soul's dark cottage, battered and decayed,
Lets in new light through chinks that time has made.

Stronger by weakness, wiser men become,

As they draw near to their eternal home.

On a Girdle.

A narrow compass! and yet there
Dwelt all that's good, and all that's fair;
Give me but what this ribbon bound,
Take all the rest the sun goes round.

Go, Lovely Rose.

How small a part of time they share
That are so wondrous sweet and fair!

To a Lady, Singing a Song of his Composing.

The eagle's fate and mine are one,
Which, on the shaft that made him die,
Espied a feather of his own,
Wherewith he wont to soar so high.

MILTON.
1608-1674.

PARADISE LOST.

Book i. Line 10.

Or if Sion hill

Delight thee more, and Siloa's brook, that flowed
Fast by the oracle of God.

Book i. Line 22.

What in me is dark,
Illumine; what is low, raise and support;
That to the height of this great argument
I may assert eternal Providence,
And justify the ways of God to men.

Book i. Line 62.

Yet from those flames
No light; but only darkness visible.

Book i. Line 65.

Where peace
And rest can never dwell: hope never comes,
That comes to all.

Book i. Line 105.

What though the field be lost?
All is not lost.

Book i. Line 254.

The mind is its own place, and in itself
Can make a heaven of hell, a hell of heaven.

Book i. Line 261.

Here we may reign secure, and in my choice
To reign is worth ambition, though in hell:
Better to reign in hell than serve in heaven.

Book i. Line 275.

Heard so oft
In worst extremes and on the perilous edge
Of battle.

Book i. Line 303.

Thick as autumnal leaves that strew the brooks
In Vallombrosa, where the Etrurian shades
High over-arched imbower.

Book i. Line 330.

Awake, arise, or be forever fallen!

Book i. Line 540.

Sonorous metal blowing martial sounds.

Book i. Line 550.

In perfect phalanx to the Dorian mood
Of flutes and soft recorders.

Book i. Line 619.

Thrice he essayed, and thrice, in spite of scorn,
Tears, such as angels weep, burst forth.

Book i. Line 742.

From morn
To noon he fell, from noon to dewy eve,
A summer's day.

Book ii. Line 113.

But all was false and hollow, though his tongue
Dropped manna; and could make the worse appear
The better reason, to perplex and dash
Maturest counsels.

Book ii. Line 300.

With grave
Aspect he rose, and in his rising seemed
A pillar of state; deep on his front engraven
Deliberation sat and public care.

Book ii. Line 306.

With Atlantean shoulders, fit to bear
The weight of mightiest monarchies: his look
Drew audience and attention still as night
Or summer's noontide air.

Book ii. Line 560.

Fixed fate, free will, foreknowledge absolute.

Book ii. Line 666.

The other shape,
If shape it might be called that shape had none
Distinguishable in member, joint, or limb.

Book ii. Line 681.

Whence and what art them, execrable shape?

Book ii. Line 846.

And Death
Grinn'd horrible a ghastly smile, to hear
His famine should be filled.

Book ii. Line 996.

With ruin upon ruin, rout on rout,
Confusion worse confounded.

Book iii. Line 1.

Hail, holy light! offspring of Heaven first-born.

Book iii. Line 44.

Or flocks, or herds, or human face divine.

Book iii. Line 495.

Since called
The Paradise of Fools, to few unknown.

Book iv. Line 34.

At whose sight all the stars
Hide their diminished heads.

Book iv. Line 76.

And in the lowest deep, a lower deep,
Still threatening to devour me, opens wide,
To which the hell I suffer seems a heaven.

Book iv. Line 108.

So farewell hope, and with hope farewell fear,
Farewell remorse; all good to me is lost:
Evil, be thou my good.

Book iv. Line 297.

For contemplation he, and valor, formed,
For softness she, and sweet attractive grace.

Book iv. Line 300.

His fair large front and eye sublime declared
Absolute rule; and hyacinthine locks
Bound from his parted forelock manly hung
Clustering, but not beneath his shoulders broad.

Book iv. Line 506.

Imparadised in one another's arms.

Book iv, Line 598.

Now came still evening on, and twilight gray
Had in her sober livery all things clad.

Book iv. Line 639.

With thee conversing, I forget all time,
All seasons and their change, all please alike.

Book iv. Line 677.

Millions of spiritual creatures walk the earth
Unseen, both when we wake and when we sleep,

Book iv. Line 750.

Hail, wedded love, mysterious law; true source
Of human happiness.

Book iv. Line 830,

Not to know me argues yourselves unknown,
The lowest of your throng.

Book v. Line 1.

Now morn, her rosy steps in the eastern clime
Advancing, sowed the earth with orient pearl.

Book v. Line 71.

Good, the more

Communicated, more abundant grows.

Book v. Line 153.

These are thy glorious works, Parent of good

Book v. Line 331,

So saying, with dispatchful look, in haste
She turns, on hospitable thoughts intent.

Book v. Line 601.

Thrones, dominations, princedoms, virtues, powers.

Book v. Line 637.

They eat, they drink, and in communion sweet
Quaff immortality and joy.

Book vi. Line 211.

Dire was the noise
Of conflict.

Book vii. Line 30.

Still govern thou my song,
Urania, and fit audience find, though few.

Book viii. Line 84.

Cycle and epicycle, orb in orb.

Book viii. Line 488.

Grace was in all her steps, heaven in her eye,
In every gesture dignity and love.

Book viii. Line 502.

Her virtue and the conscience of her worth,
That would be wooed and not unsought be won.

Book viii. Line 548.

So well to know
Her own, that what she wills to do or say
Seems wisest, virtuousest, discreetest, best!

Book viii. Line 600.

Those graceful acts,
Those thousand decencies, that daily flow
From all her words and actions.

Book viii. Line 618.

To whom the angel, with a smile that glowed
Celestial rosy red (love's proper Hue)

Book ix. Line 249.

For solitude sometimes is best society,
And short retirement urges sweet return.

Book x. Line 77.

Yet I shall temper so
Justice with mercy, as may illustrate most
Them fully satisfied, and thee appease.

Book xii. Line 646.

The world was all before them, where to choose
Their place of rest, and Providence their guide.

PARADISE REGAINED.

Book iv Line 240.

Athens, the eye of Greece, mother of arts
And eloquence.

Book iv. Line 267.

Thence to the famous orators repair,
Those ancient, whose resistless eloquence
Wielded at will that fierce democraty,
Shook the arsenal, and fulmined over Greece,
To Macedon, and Artaxerxes' throne.

Book iv. Line 330.

As children gathering pebbles on the shore.

SAMSON AGONISTES.

Line 293.

Just are the ways of God,
And justifiable to men.

Line 1350.

He's gone, and who knows how he may report
Thy words, by adding fuel to the flame?

COMUS.

Line 205.

A thousand fantasies
Begin to throng into my memory,
Of calling shapes and beckoning shadows dire,
And airy tongues, that syllable men's names
On sands, and shores, and desert wildernesses.

Line 221.

Was I deceived, or did a sable cloud
Turn forth her silver lining on the night?

Line 244.

Can any mortal mixture of earth's mould
Breathe such divine, enchanting ravishment?

Line 256.

Who, as they sung, would take the prisoned soul
And lap it in Elysium.

Line 381.

He that has light within his own clear breast
May sit i' th' center and enjoy bright day;
But he that hides a dark soul and foul thoughts
Benighted walks under the midday sun,

Line 476.

How charming is divine philosophy!
Not harsh and crabbed, as dull fools suppose;
But musical as is Apollo's lute,
And a perpetual feast of nectared sweets,
Where no crude surfeit reigns.

Line 560.

I was all ear,
And took in strains that might create a soul
Under the rib of Death.

LYCIDAS.

Line 10.

He knew
Himself to sing, and build the lofty rhyme.

Line 14.

Without the meed of some melodious tear.

Line 70.

Fame is the spur that the clear spirit doth raise
(That last infirmity of noble minds)
To scorn delights and live laborious days;
But the fair guerdon when we hope to find,
And think to burst out into sudden blaze,
Comes the blind Fury with the abhorred shears
And slits the thin-spun life.

Line 101.

Built in the eclipse and rigged with curses dark.

Line 109.

The pilot of the Galilean lake.

Line 168.

So sinks the day-star in the ocean bed,
And yet anon repairs his drooping head,
And tricks his beams, with new spangled ore
Flames in the forehead of the morning sky.

Line 198.

To-morrow to fresh woods and pastures new.
L'ALLEGRO.

Line 27.

Quips and cranks, and wanton wiles,
Nods and becks, and wreathed smiles.

Line 33.

Come, and trip it as you go,

On the light, fantastic toe.

Line 67.

And every shepherd tells his tale
Under the hawthorn in the dale.

Line 79.

Where perhaps some beauty lies,
The Cynosure of neighboring eyes.

Line 117.

Towered cities please us then,
And the busy hum of men.

Line 133.

Or sweetest Shakespeare, Fancy's child,
Warble his native wood-notes wild.

Line 136.

Lap me in soft Lydian airs,
Married to immortal verse,
Such as the meeting soul may pierce
In notes, with many a winding bout

Of linked sweetness long drawn out.
IL PENSEROSO.

Line 39.

And looks commercing with the skies,
Thy rapt soul sitting in thine eyes.

Line 61.

Sweet bird, that shunn'st the noise of folly,
Most musical, most melancholy!

Line 106.

Such notes, as, warbled to the string,
Drew iron tears down Pluto's cheek.

Line 120.

Where more is meant than meets the ear.

Line 159.

And storied windows richly dight,
Casting a dim, religious light.

Sonnet to the Lady Margaret Ley.

That old man eloquent.

Sonnet on his Blindness.

They also serve who only stand and wait.

Second Sonnet to Cyriac Skinner.

Yet I argue not
Against Heaven's hand or will, nor bate a jot
Of heart or hope; but still bear up and steer
Right onward.

Sonnet on his Deceased Wife.

But oh! as to embrace me she inclined,
I waked; she fled; and day brought back my night.

SAMUEL BUTLER.
1612-1680.

Hudibras.

Part i. Canto i. Line 51

Besides, 'tis known he could speak Greek
As naturally as pigs squeak.

Part i. Canto i. Line 67

He could distinguish, and divide
A hair, 'twixt south and southwest side.

Part i. Canto i. Line 81

For rhetoric, he could not ope
His mouth, but out there flew a trope.

Part i. Canto i. Line 131.

Whatever sceptic could inquire for,
For every why he had a wherefore.

Part i. Canto i. Line 149

He knew whit's what, and that's as high
As metaphysic wit can fly.

Part i. Canto i. Line 199

And prove their doctrine orthodox
By Apostolic blows and knocks.

Part i. Canto i. Line 215

Compound for sins they are inclined to,

By damning those they have no mind to.

Part i. Canto i. Line 463

For rhyme the rudder is of verses,
With which, like ships, they steer their
courses.

Part i. Canto i. Line 489

He ne'er considered it, as loth
To look a gift-horse in the mouth.

Part i. Canto i. Line 821

Quoth Hudibras, "I smell a rat;
Ralpho, thou dost prevaricate."

Part i. Canto i. Line 852

Or shear swine, all cry and no wool.

Part i. Canto ii. Line 633

And bid the devil take the hin'most,
Which at this race is like to win most.

Part i. Canto ii. Line 831

With many a stiff thwack, many a bang,
Hard crab-tree and old iron rang.

Part i. Canto iii. Line 1

Ay me! what perils do environ
The man that meddles with cold iron.

Part i. Canto iii. Line 263

Nor do I know what is become
Of him, more than the Pope of Rome.

Part i. Canto iii. Line 309

H' had got a hurt
O' th' inside of a deadlier sort.

Part i. Canto iii. Line 877

I am not now in fortune's power;
He that is down can fall no lower.

Part i. Canto iii. Line 1367

Thou hast

Outrun the Constable at last.

Part ii. Canto i. Line 29

For one for sense, and one for rhyme,
I think's sufficient at one time.

Part ii. Canto i. Line 465

For what is worth in anything,
But so much money as 'twill bring.

Part ii. Canto n. Line 29

The sun had long since in the lap
Of Thetis taken out his nap,
And, like a lobster boiled, the morn
From black to red began to turn.

Part ii. Canto ii. Line 79

Have always been at daggers-drawing.
And one another clapper-clawing.

Part ii. Canto ii Line 503

And look before you ere you leap;
For as you sow, y' are like to reap.

Part ii. Canto iii. Line 1.

Doubtless the pleasure is as great
Of being cheated, as to cheat.

Part ii. Canto iii. Line 261.

He made an instrument to know
If the moon shine at full or no....
And prove that she's not made of green cheese.[6]

[Note 6: "The moon is made of a green cheese"
Jack Jugler, p. 46.]

Part ii. Canto iii. Line 580

You have a wrong sow by the ear.

Part ii. Canto iii. Line 923

To swallow gudgeons ere they're catched,
And count their chickens ere they're hatched.

Part ii. Canto iii. Line 1067

As quick as lightning, in the breach
Just in the place where honor 's lodged,
As wise philosophers have judged,
Because a kick in that place more
Hurts honor than deep wounds before,

Part iii. Canto i. Line 3

As he that has two strings t' his bow.

Part iii. Canto ii. Line 175.

True as the dial to the sun,
Although it be not sinned upon.

Part iii. Canto iii. Line 243

For those that fly may fight again,
Which he can never do that's slain.

Part iii. Canto iii. Line 547

He that complies against his will
Is of his own opinion still.

MARQUIS OF MONTROSE.
1612-1650.

Song, "My Dear and only Love."

I'll make thee famous by my pen,
And glorious by my sword.

DRYDEN.
1631-1700.

Alexander's feast.

Line 15.

None but the brave deserves the fair.

Line 60.

Sweet is pleasure after pain.

Line 66.

Soothed with the sound, the king grew vain;
Fought all his battles o'er again;
And thrice he routed all his foes; and thrice
he slew the slain.

Line 78,

Fallen from his high estate,
And weltering in his blood;
Deserted, at his utmost need,
By those his former bounty fed;

On the bare earth exposed he lies,
With not a friend to close his eyes.

Line 96.

For pity melts the mind to love.

Line 99.

War, he sung, is toil and trouble;
Honor, but an empty bubble.

Line 106.

Take the good the gods provide thee.

Line 120

Sighed and looked, and sighed again.

Line 154.

And, like another Helen, fired another Troy.

Line 160.

Could swell the soul to rage, or kindle soft desire.

Line 169.

He raided a mortal to the skies
She drew an angel down.

Cymon and Iphigenia.

Line 84.

He trudged along, unknowing what he sought,
And whistled as he went, for want of thought.

Absalom and Achitophet.

A fiery soul, which, working out its way
Fretted the pigmy body to decay,
And o'er informed the tenement of clay.

Part i. Line 363

Great wits are sure to madness near allied,
And thin partitions do their bounds divide.

Part i. Line 174

Resolved to ruin or to rule the state.

Part i. Line 534

Who think too little, and who talk too much

Part i. Line 545

A man so various, that he seemed to be
Not one, but all mankind's epitome;
Stiff in opinions, always in the wrong,
Was everything by starts, and nothing long.

Part i. Line 1005

Beware the fury of a patient man.

Part ii. Line 463

For every inch, that is not fool, is rogue.

All for Love. Prologue.

Errors like straws upon the surface flow;
He who would search for pearls must dive below.

Act iv. Sc. 1.

Men are but children of a larger growth.

Conquest of Grenada. Part i. Sc. 1.

I am as free as nature first made man,
Ere the base laws of servitude began,
When wild in woods the noble savage ran.

Spanish Friar. Act ii. Sc. 1.

There is a pleasure
In being mad which none but madmen know.

Don Sebastian. Act i. Sc. 1.

This is the porcelain clay of human kind.

Translation of Juvenal's 10th Satire.

Look round the habitable world, how few
Know their own good, or, knowing it, pursue.

Prologue to Lee's Sophonisba.

Thespis, the first professor of our art,
At country wakes sung ballads from a cart.

Imitation of the 29th of Horace.

Book i. Line 65.

Happy the man, and happy he alone,
He, who can call to-day his own:

He who, secure within, can say,
To-morrow do thy worst, for I have lived to-day.

On Milton.

Three Poets, in three distant ages born,
Greece, Italy, and England did adorn;
The first in loftiness of thought surpassed,
The next in majesty, in both the last.
The force of nature could no further go;
To make a third she joined the other two.

JOHN BUNYAN.
1628-1688.

Apology for his Book.

And so I penned
It down, until at last it came to be,
For length and breadth, the bigness which you see.
Some said, "John, print it," others said,
"Not so."
Some said, "It might do good," others said,
"No."

Pilgrim's Progress.

The Slough of Despond.

EARL OF ROSCOMMON.
1633-1684.

Essay on Translated Verse.

Immodest words admit of no defence,
For want of decency is want of sense.

EARL OF ROCHESTER.

Written on the Bedchamber Door of Charles II.

Here lies our sovereign lord the king,
Whose word no man relies on;
He never says a foolish thing,
Nor ever does a wise one.

KING CHARLES II.

Written in Parliament attending the Discussion of Lord Boss' Divorce Bill.

As good as a play.

SHEFFIELD, DUKE OF BUCKINGHAMSHIRE.
1649-1721.

Essay on Poetry.

Of all those arts in which the wise excel,
Nature's chief masterpiece is writing well.

There's no such thing in nature, and you'll draw
A faultless monster, which the world ne'er saw.
Read Homer once, and you can read no more,
For all books else appear so mean, so poor;
Verse will seem prose; but still persist to read,
And Homer will be all the books you need.

THOMAS OTWAY.
1651-1685.

Venice Preserved.

Act i. Sc. 1.

O woman! lovely woman! Nature made thee
To temper man; we had been brutes without you.
Angels are painted fair to look like you.

JOHN NORRIS.
1657-1711.

The Parting.

How fading are the joys we dote upon!
Like apparitions seen and gone;
But those which soonest take their flight
Are the most exquisite and strong;
Like angel's visits, short and bright,
Mortality's too weak to bear them long.

NATHANIEL LEE.
1655-1692.

Alexander the Great.

Act i. Sc. 3.

Then he will talk--ye gods, how he will talk!

Act iv. Sc. 2.

When Greeks joined Greeks, then was the tug of war.

TOM BROWN.
--1704.

Dialogues of the Dead.

I do not love thee, Doctor Fell,
The reason why I cannot tell;
But this alone I know full well,
I do not love thee, Doctor Fell.[7]

[Note 7: "Non amo te, Sabidi, nee possum dicere quare;
Hoc tautum possum dicere, non amo te."
Martial, Ep. I. xxxiii.]

THOMAS SOUTHERN.
1659-1746.

Oroonoka.

Act ii. Sc. 1.

Pity's akin to love.

DANIEL DEFOE.
1661-1731.

The True-Born Englishman.

Part i. Line 1

Wherever God erects a house of prayer,
The Devil always builds a chapel there;
And 'twill be found upon examination,
The latter has the largest congregation.

LOUIS THEOBALD.
1688-1744.

The Double Falsehood.

None but himself can be his parallel.

MATTHEW PRIOR.
1664-1721.

English Padlock.

Be to her virtues very kind;
Be to her faults a little blind.

Henry and Emma.

That air and harmony of shape express,
Fine by degrees, and beautifully less.

The Thief and the Cordelier.

Now fitted the halter, now traversed the cart,
And often took leave; but was loth to depart.

Epilogue to Lucius.

And the gray mare will prove the better horse.[8]

[Note 8: See Hudibras, Part ii. Canto ii. line 698. Mr. Macaulay
thinks that this proverb originated in the preference generally given to
the gray mares of Flanders over the finest coach-horses of
England.--History of England, Vol. I. Ch. 3.]

Imitations of Horace.

Of two evils I have chose the least.

Epitaph on Himself.

Here lies what once was Matthew Prior;
The son of Adam and of Eve:
Can Bourbon or Nassau claim higher?

Ode in Imitation of Horace. B. iii. Od. 2.

And virtue is her own reward.

COLLEY CIBBER.
1671-1757.

Richard III.

Act iv. Sc. 3.

Off with his head! so much for Buckingham!

Act v. Sc. 3.

Richard is himself again!

JOSEPH ADDISON.
1672-1719.

CATO.

Act i. Sc. 1.

The dawn is overcast, the morning lowers,
And heavily in clouds brings on the day,
The great, th' important day, big with the fate
Of Cato, and of Home.

Act i. Sc. 1.

Thy steady temper, Portius,
Can look on guilt, rebellion, fraud, and Caesar,
In the calm lights of mild philosophy.

Act i. Sc. 1.

'Tis not in mortals to command success,
But we'll do more, Sempronius: we'll deserve it.

Act i. Sc. 1.

'Tis pride, rank pride, and haughtiness of soul;

I think the Romans call it Stoicism.

Act i. Sc. 1.

Were you with these, my prince, you'd soon forget
The pale unripened beauties of the North.

Act ii. Sc. 1.

My voice is still for war.
Gods! can a Roman Senate long debate
Which of the two to choose, slavery or death?

Act iv. Sc. 1.

The woman that deliberates is lost.

Act iv. Sc. 2.

When vice prevails, and impious men bear sway,
The post of honor is a private station.

Act v. Sc. 1.

It must be so.--Plato, thou reasonest well.
Else whence this pleasing hope, this fond desire,
This longing after immortality?
'Tis the Divinity that stirs within us;

'Tis Heaven itself that points out an hereafter,
And intimates Eternity to man.

Act v. Sc. I.

I'm weary of conjectures.

Act v. Sc. 1.

The soul secured in her existence, smiles
At the drawn dagger, and defies its point.

Act v. Sc. 1.

The wreck of matter, and the crush of worlds

The Campaign.

And, pleased th' Almighty's orders to perform
Rides in the whirlwind and directs the storm.[9]
[Note 9: This line has been frequently ascribed to Pope, as it is
found in the Dunciad, Book iii., line 261.]

From the Letter on Italy.

For wheresoe'er I turn my ravished eyes,
Gay gilded scenes and shining prospects rise;
Poetic fields encompass me around,
And still I seem to tread on classic ground.[10]

[Note 10: Malone states that this was the first time the phrase classic ground, since so common, was ever used.]

Ode.

The spacious firmament on high,
With all the blue, ethereal sky,
And spangled heavens, a shining frame,
Their great Original proclaim.
Soon as the evening shades prevail,
The moon takes up the wondrous tale,
And nightly to the listening earth
Repeats the story of her birth;
While all the stars that round her burn,
And all the planets in their tarn,
Confirm the tidings as they roll,
And spread the truth from pole to pole.
Forever singing, as they shine,
The hand that made us is divine.

JONATHAN SWIFT.
1667-1745.

Imitation of Horace. B. ii. Sat. 6.

I've often wished that I had clear,
For life, six hundred pounds a year,
A handsome house to lodge a friend,

A river at my garden's end.

Poetry, a Rhapsody.

So geographers, in Afric maps,
With savage pictures fill their gaps,
And o'er unhabitable downs
Place elephants for want of towns.

WILLIAM CONGREVE.
1669-1729.

The Mourning Bride. Act i. Sc. 1.

Music hath charms to soothe the savage breast.
To soften rocks, or bend a knotted oak.
By magic numbers and persuasive sound.

Act iii. Sc. 1.

Heaven has no rage like love to hatred turned,
Nor Hell a fury like a woman scorned.

ALEXANDER POPE.
1688-1744.

ESSAY ON MAN.

Epistle i. Line 5.

Expatiate free o'er all this scene of man;
A mighty maze! but not without a plan.

Line 13.

Eye nature's walks, shoot folly as it flies,
And catch the manners living as they rise.

Line 88.

A hero perish or a sparrow fall.

Line 95.

Hope springs eternal in the human breast:
Man never *is*, but always *to be* blest.

Line 99.

Lo, the poor Indian! whose untutored mind
Sees God in clouds, or hears him in the wind.

Line 200.

Die of a rose in aromatic pain?

Line 294.

One truth is clear, Whatever is, is right.

Epistle ii. Line 1.

Know then thyself, presume not God to scan;
The proper study of mankind is man.[11]

[Note 11: From Charron (de la Sagesse):--"La vraye science et
le vray etude de l'homme c'est l'homme."]

Line 217.

Vice is a monster of so frightful mien,
As to be hated, needs but to be seen;
But seen too oft, familiar with her face,
We first endure, then pity, then embrace.

Line 231.

Virtuous and vicious every man must be,
Few in th' extreme, but all in the degree.

Line 276.

Pleased with a rattle, tickled with a straw.
Epistle iii. Line 305.
For modes of faith let graceless zealots fight;
His can't be wrong whose life is in the right.
Epistle iv. Line 49.
Order is Heaven's first law.

Line 193.

Honor and shame from no condition rise;
Act well your part--there all the honor lies.

Line 203.

Worth makes the man, and want of it the fellow;
The rest is all but leather or prunella.

Line 215.

What can ennoble sots, or slaves, or cowards?
Alas! not all the blood of all the Howards.

Line 247.

A wit's a feather, and a chief a rod;
An honest man's the noblest work of God.

Line 254.

Plays round the head, but comes not to the heart.

Line 281.

Think how Bacon shined,
The wisest, brightest, meanest of mankind.

Line 310.

Virtue alone is happiness below.

Line 330.

Slave to no sect, who takes no private road,
But looks through nature up to nature's God.

Line 379.

Formed by thy converse happily to steer
Prom grave to gay, from lively to severe.

MORAL ESSAYS.

Epistle i. Line 135.

'Tis from high life high characters are drawn--
A saint in crape is twice a saint in lawn.

Line 149.

'Tis education forms the common mind:
Just as the twig is bent, the tree's inclined.

Line 246.

Odious! in woollen! 'twould a saint provoke,
Were the last words that poor Narcissa spoke.
Epistle ii. Line 15.
Whether the charmers sinner it or saint it,
If folly grow romantic, I must paint it.

Line 43.

Fine by defect and delicately weak.

Line 97.

With too much quickness ever to be taught,

With too much thinking to have common thought.

Line 215.

Men, some to business, some to pleasure take;
But every woman is at heart a rake.

Line 268.

And mistress of herself, though china fall.

Line 270.

Woman's at best a contradiction still.
Epistle iii. Line 1.
Who shall decide when doctors disagree?

Line 95.

But thousands die without or this or that,
Die, and endow a college or a cat.

Line 153.

The ruling passion, be it what it will,
The ruling passion conquers reason still.

Line 161.

Extremes in nature equal good produce.

Line 250.

Rise, honest muse! and sing--The man of Ross.

Line 285.

Who builds a church to God, and not to fame,
Will never mark the marble with his name.

AN ESSAY ON CRITICISM.

Part i. Line 9.

'Tis with our judgments as our watches; none
Go just alike, yet each believes his own.

Line 153.

And snatch a grace beyond the reach of art.

Part ii. Line 215.

A little learning is a dangerous thing.
Drink deep, or taste not the Pierian spring.

Line 232.

Hills peep o'er hills, and Alps on Alps arise,

Line 297.

True wit is nature to advantage dressed,
What oft was thought, but ne'er so well expressed.

Line 357.

That, like a wounded snake, drags its slow length along.

Line 362.

True ease in writing comes from art, not chance,
As those move easiest who have learned to dance.

Line 365.

The sound must seem an echo to the sense.

Line 525.

To err is human: to forgive, divine.

Part iii. Line 625.

For fools rush in where angels fear to tread.

ELEGY TO THE MEMORY OF AN UNFORTUNATE LADY.

Line 54.

By strangers honored and by strangers mourned
And bear about the mockery of woe
To midnight dances and the public show.

THE RAPE OF THE LOCK.

Canto ii. Line 7.

On her white breast a sparkling cross she wore,
Which Jews might kiss and infidels adore.

Canto ii. Line 17.

If to her share some female errors fall,
Look on her face, and you'll forget them all.

Canto iii. Line 16.

At every word a reputation dies.

Line 21.

The hungry judges soon the sentence sign,
And wretches hang, that jurymen may dine.

SATIRES AND IMITATIONS OF HORACE

Prologue, Line 1.
Shut, shut the door, good John.

Line 12.

E'en Sunday shines no Sabbath day to me.

Line 18.

Who pens a stanza when he should engross.

Line 127.

As yet a child, nor yet a fool to fame,
I lisped in numbers, for the numbers came.

Line 197.

Should such a man, too fond to rule alone,
Bear, like the Turk, no brother near the throne,

Line 201.

Damn with faint praise, assent with civil leer,
And without sneering teach the rest to sneer.

Line 308.

Who breaks a butterfly upon a wheel?

Line 333.

Wit that can creep, and pride that licks the dust.
Book ii. Satire i. Line 6.
Lord Fanny spins a thousand such a day.

Line 69.

Satire's my weapon, but I'm too discreet

To run a muck, and tilt at all I meet.

Line 127.

Then St. John mingles with my friendly bowl,
The feast of reason and the flow of soul.

Book ii. Satire ii. Line 159.

For I, who hold sage Homer's rule the best,
Welcome the coming, speed the going guest.[12]

[Note 12: See the Odyssey, Book xv. line 83.]

Book ii. Epistle i. Line 108.

The mob of gentlemen who wrote with ease.

Epilogue to the Satires.

Dialogue i. Line 136.

Do good by stealth, and blush to find it fame.

Epitaph on Gay.

Of manners gentle, of affections mild;
In wit a man, simplicity a child.

THE DUNCIAD.

Book i. Line 54.

And solid pudding against empty praise.

Book iii. Line 158.

All crowd, who foremost shall be damned to fame.

Book iii. Line 165.

Silence, ye wolves! while Ralph to Cynthia howls,
And makes night hideous; answer him, ye owls.

Book iv. Line 614.

E'en Palinurus nodded at the helm.

ODYSSEY.

Book ii. Line 315.

Few sons attain the praise
Of their great sires, and most their sires disgrace.

Book xiv. Line 410.

Far from gay cities and the ways of men.

Book xv. Line 79.

Who love too much, hate in the like extreme.

Book xv. Line 83.

True friendship's laws are by this rule expressed,
Welcome the coming, speed the parting guest.

Windsor forest.

Thus, if small things we may with great compare.

Martinus Scriblerus on the Art of Sinking in Poetry.

Chapter xi.

Ye Gods! annihilate but space and time,
And make two lovers happy.

Epitaph on the Hon. S. Harcourt.

Who ne'er knew joy but friendship might divide,
Or gave his father grief but when he died.

THOMAS TICKELL.
1686-1740.

On the Death of Addison. Line 45.

Nor e'er was to the bowers of bliss conveyed
A fairer spirit, or more welcome shade.

Line 79.

There taught us how to live; and (oh! too high
The price for knowledge) taught us how to die.

Colin and Lucy.

I hear a voice you cannot hear,
Which says I must not stay,
I see a hand you cannot see,
Which beckons me away.

JOHN GAY.
1688-1732.

What D'ye Call 't.

Act ii. Sc. 9.

So comes a reckoning when the banquet's o'er,
The dreadful reckoning, and men smile no more.

Beggars' Opera.

Act i. Sc. 1.

O'er the hills and far away.
How happy could I be with either,
Were t'other dear charmer away.

FABLES.

The Shepherd and the Philosopher.

Whence is thy learning? Hath thy toil
O'er books consumed the midnight oil?

The Mother, the Nurse, and the Fairy.

When yet was ever found a mother
Who'd give her booby for another?

The Sick Man and the Angel.

While there is life there's hope, he cried.

The Hare and Many Friends.

And when a lady's in the case,
You know all other things give place.

Epitaph on Himself.

Life's a jest, and all things show it;
I thought so once, and now I know it.

LADY MARY WORTLEY MONTAGUE.
1690-1762.

The Lady's Resolve.

Let this great maxim be my virtue's guide--
In part she is to blame that has been tried;
He comes too near, that comes to be denied.

NICHOLAS ROWE.
1673-1718.

The Fair Penitent.

Act ii. Sc. 1.

Is she not more than painting can express,
Or youthful poets fancy when they love?

Act v. Sc. 1.

Is this that gallant, gay Lothario?

JOHN PHILIPS.
1676-1708.

Splendid Shilling.

Line 121.

My galligaskins, that have long withstood
The winter's fury and encroaching frosts,

By time subdued (what will not time subdue?)
A horrid chasm disclosed.

THOMAS PARNELL.
1679-1718.

The Hermit. Line 5.

Remote from men, with God he passed his days,
Prayer all his business, all his pleasure praise.

BARTON BOOTH.
1681-1733.

Song.

True as the needle to the pole,
Or as the dial to the sun.

MATTHEW GREEN.
1696-1737.

The Spleen. Line 93.

Fling but a stone, the giant dies.

JOHN BYROM.
1691-1763.

'On the Feuds between Handel and Bononcini.[13]

Some say, compared to Bononcini,
That Mynheer Handel's but a ninny;
Others aver that he to Handel
Is scarcely fit to hold a candle.
Strange all this difference should be
'Twixt Tweedledum and Tweedledee.

[Note 13: "Nourse asked me if I had seen the verses upon Handel and
Bononcini, not knowing that they were mine." Byrom's Remains (Chelten-
ham
Soc), Vol. I. p 173. The last two lines have been attributed to Switt
and Pope. *Vide* Scott's edition of Swift, and Dyce's edition of Pope.]

The Astrologer.

As clear as a whistle.

Epigram on Two Monopolists.

Bone and skin, two millers thin,
Would starve us all, or near it;
But be it known to Skin and Bone
That Flesh and Blood can't bear it.

BISHOP BERKELEY.
1684-1753.

On the Prospect of Planting Arts and Learning in America.

Westward the course of empire takes its way;
The four first acts already past,
A fifth shall close the drama with the day;
Time's noblest offspring is the last.

ROBERT BLAIR.
1699-1746.

The Grave. Part ii. Line 586.

The good he scorned,
Stalked off reluctant, like an ill-used ghost,
Not to return; or if it did, in visits
Like those of angels, short and far between.

EDWARD YOUNG.
1681-1765.

NIGHT THOUGHTS.

Night i. Line 1.

Tired Nature's sweet restorer, balmy sleep!

Night i. Line 55.

The bell strikes one. We take no note of time
But from its loss.

Night i. Line 154.

To waft a feather or to drown a fly.

Night i. Line 390.

Be wise to-day; 'tis madness to defer.

Night i. Line 393.

Procrastination is the thief of time.

Night i. Line 417.

At thirty man suspects himself a fool;
Knows it at forty, and reforms his plan.

Night i. Line 424.

All men think all men mortal but themselves.

Night ii. Line 376.

'Tis greatly wise to talk with our past hours,
And ask them what report they bore to heaven.

Night ii. Line 602.

How blessings brighten as they take their flight!

Night ii. Line 633.

The chamber where the good man meets his fate
Is privileged beyond the common walk
Of virtuous life, quite in the verge of heaven.

Night iii. Line 81.

Beautiful as sweet!
And young as beautiful! and soft as young!
And gay as soft! and innocent as gay!

Night iii. Line 104

Lovely in death the beauteous ruin lay.

Night iv. Line 10.

The knell, the shroud, the mattock, and the grave,
The deep, damp vault, the darkness, and the worm.

Night iv. Line 15.

Man makes a death, which nature never made.

Night iv. Line 118.

Man wants but little, nor that little long.

Night v. Line 775.

The man of wisdom is the man of years.

Night v. Line 1011.

Death loves a shining mark, a signal blow.

Night vi. Line 309.

Pygmies are pygmies still, though perched on Alps.
And pyramids are pyramids in vales.

Night vi. Line 606.

And all may do what has by man been done.

Night vii. Line 496.

The man that blushes is not quite a brute.

Night ix. Line 771.

An undevout astronomer is mad.

Night ix. Line 1660.

Emblazed to seize the sight; who runs, may read.

LOVE OF FAME.

Satire i. Line 89.

Some, for renown, on scraps of learning dote,
And think they grow immortal as they quote.

Satire i. Line 238.

None think the great unhappy, but the great.

Satire ii. Line 207.

Where nature's end of language is declined,
And men talk only to conceal their mind.[14]

[Note 14: "Ils n'emploient les paroles que pour deguiser leurs pensees "--Voltaire.]

Satire vii. Line 97.

How commentators each dark passage shun,
And hold their farthing candle to the sun.[15]

[Note 15: Imitated by Crabbe in the Parish Register, Part I.,
Introduction, and taken originally from Burton's Anatomy of Melancholy,
Part III. Sec. 2. Mem. 1. Subs 2. "But to enlarge or illustrate this
power or effects of love is to set a candle in the sun."]

Lines Written with the Diamond Pencil of Lord Chesterfield.

Accept a miracle, instead of wit,
See two dull lines with Stanhope's pencil writ.

HENRY CAREY.
1663-1743.

God save the King.[16]

God save our gracious king,
Long live our noble king,
God save the king.

[Note 16: The authorship both of the words and music of "God save the
King" has long been a matter of dispute, and is still unsettled, though
the weight of the evidence is in favor of Carey's claim.]

Chrononhotonthologos. Act i. Sc. 3.

To thee, and gentle Rigdum Funnidos,
Our gratulations flow in streams unbounded.

Act ii. Sc. 4.

Go call a coach, and let a coach be called,
And let the man who calleth be the caller;
And in his calling let him nothing call
But Coach! Coach! Coach! O for a coach, ye gods!

ISAAC WATTS.
1674-1748.

DIVINE SONGS.

To God the Father, God the Son,
And God the Spirit, three in one,
Be honor, praise, and glory given,
By all on earth, and all in heaven.
Hush! my dear, lie still and slumber
Holy angels guard thy bed!
Heavenly blessings without number
Gently falling on thy head.
Let dogs delight to bark and bite,
For God hath made them so;
Let bears and lions growl and fight.

For 'tis their nature too.
How doth the little busy bee
Improve each shining hour,
And gather honey all the day,
From every opening flower.
Hark! from the tombs a doleful sound.
'Tis the voice of the sluggard, I heard him complain,
"You have waked me too soon, I must slumber again."

SIR SAMUEL TUKE.
--1673.

Adventures of Five Hours. Act v. Sc. 3.

He is a fool who thinks by force or skill
To turn the current of a woman's will.

AARON HILL
1685-1750.

Epilogue to Zara.

First, then, a woman will, or won't--depend on 't;
If she will do 't, she will; and there's an end on 't.

But, if she won't, since safe and sound your trust is,
Fear is affront: and jealousy injustice.[17]

Verses Written on a Window in Scotland.

Tender-handed stroke a nettle,
And it stings you for your pains;
Grasp it like a man of mettle,
And it soft as silk remains.

[Note 17: The following lines are copied from the pillar erected on
the mount in the Dane John Field, Canterbury:
"Where is the man who has the power and skill
To stem the torrent of a woman's will?
For if she will, she will, you may depend on 't;
And if she won't, she won't; so there's an end on't."]

'Tis the same with common natures:
Use 'em kindly, they rebel;
But be rough as nutmeg-graters,
And the rogues obey you well.

RICHARD SAVAGE.
1698-1743.

The Bastard. Line 7.

He lives to build, not boast a generous race:

No tenth transmitter of a foolish face.

JAMES THOMSON.
1700-1748.

THE SEASONS.

Spring. Line 283.

Base envy withers at another's joy,
And hates that excellence it cannot reach.

Line 465.

But who can paint
Like Nature? Can imagination boast,
Amid its gay creation, hues like hers?

Line 1149.

Delightful task! to rear the tender thought,--
To teach the young idea how to shoot,--

Line 1158.

An elegant sufficiency, content,
Retirement, rural quiet, friendship, books.
Ease and alternate labor, useful life,
Progressive virtue, and approving Heaven!

Summer. Line 1188.

Sighed and looked unutterable things.

Line 1285.

A lucky chance, that oft decides the fate
Of mighty monarchs.

Line 1346.

So stands the statue that enchants the world.

Autumn. Line 204.

Loveliness
Needs not the foreign aid of ornament,
But is when unadorned, adorned the most.

Line 283.

For still the world prevailed, and its dread laugh,
Which scarce the firm philosopher can scorn.

Winter. Line 393.

Cruel as death, and hungry as the grave.

Hymn. Line 25.

Shade, unperceived, so softening into shade.

Line 114.

From seeming evil still educing good.

Line 118.

Come then, expressive silence, muse his praise.

Castle of Indolence. Canto i. St. 69.

A little round, fat, oily man of God.

Alfred. Act ii. Sc. 5.

Rule Britannia, Britannia rules the waves;
Britons never will be slaves.

Song, "Forever, Fortune."

Forever, Fortune, wilt thou prove
An unrelenting foe to love;
And, when we meet a mutual heart,
Step rudely in, and bid us part?

Sophonisba. Act iii. Sc. 2.

O Sophonisba! Sophonisba, O![18]

[Note 18: This line was altered, after the second edition, to "O Sophonisba! I am wholly thine."]

JOHN DYER.
1700-1758.

Grongar Hill. Line 163.

Ever charming, ever new,
When will the landscape tire the view.

Line 123.

As yon summits soft and fair,
Clad in colors of the air,
Which to those who journey near
Barren, brown, and rough appear.

PHILIP DODDRIDGE.
1702-1751.

Epigram on his Family Arms.

Live while you live, the epicure would say,
And seize the pleasures of the present day;
Live while you live, the sacred preacher cries,
And give to God each moment as it flies.
Lord, in my views let both united be;
I live in pleasure, when I live to thee.

ROBERT DODSLEY
1703-1764.

The Parting Kiss.

One kind kiss before we part,
Drop a tear and bid adieu;
Though we sever, my fond heart
Till we meet shall pant for you.

SAMUEL JOHNSON.
1709-1784.

Prologue on the Opening of Drury Lane Theatre.

Each exchange of many-colored life he drew,
Exhausted worlds, and then imagined new,
And panting time toiled after him in vain.
For we that live to please must please to live.

Vanity of Human Wishes.

Line 1.

Let observation with extensive view
Survey mankind, from China to Peru.[19]

[Note 19: The Universal Love of Pleasure, line 1: "All human race, from China to Peru, Pleasure, however disguised by art, pursue." ***Rev. Thos. Warton***.]

Line 159.

There mark what ills the scholar's life assail--
Toil, envy, want, the patron, and the jail.

Line 221.

He left the name, at which the world grew pale,
To point a moral, or adorn a tale.

Line 257.

Hides from himself his state, and shuns to know
That life protracted is protracted woe.

Line 306.

Superfluous lags the veteran on the stage.

Line 318.

And Swift expires, a driveller and a show.

Line 346.

Roll darkling down the torrent of his fate.

London. Line 166.

Of all the griefs that harass the distressed,
Sure the most bitter is a scornful jest.

Line 176.

This mournful truth is everywhere confessed,
Slow rises worth by poverty depressed.

Lines added to Goldsmith's Traveller.

How small, of all that human hearts endure,
That part which laws or kings can cause or cure!
Still to ourselves in every place consigned,
Our own felicity we make or find.
With secret course, which no loud storms annoy,
Glides the smooth current of domestic joy.

Line added to Goldsmith's Deserted Village.

Trade's proud empire hastes to swift decay.

From Dr. Madden's "Boulter's Monument."

Supposed to have been inserted by Dr. Johnson. 1745.

Words are men's daughters, but God's sons are things.

Basselas. Chapter i.

Ye who listen with credulity to the whispers
of fancy, and pursue with eagerness the phantoms
of hope; who expect that age will perform
the promises of youth, and that the deficiencies
of the present day will be supplied by
the morrow; attend to the history of Rasselas,

Prince of Abyssinia.

Epitaph on Robert Levett.

In Misery's darkest cavern known,
His useful care was ever nigh,
Where hopeless Anguish poured his groan,
And lonely Want retired to die.

Epitaph on Claudius Phillips, the Musician.

Phillips, whose touch harmonious could remove
The pangs of guilty power or hapless love;
Rest here, distressed by poverty no more,
Here find that calm thou gav'st so oft before;
Sleep, undisturbed, within this peaceful shrine,
Till angels wake thee with a note like thine.

LORD LYTTELTON
1709-1773.

Prologue to Thomson's Coriolanus.

For his chaste Muse employed her heaven-taught lyre
None but the noblest passions to inspire,
Not one immoral, one corrupted thought,
One line, which dying he could wish to blot.

Epigram.

None without hope e'er loved the brightest fair,
But love can hope where reason would despair.

Soliloquy on a Beauty in the Country.

Where none admire, 'tis useless to excel;
Where none are beaux, 'tis vain to be a belle.

Song.

Alas! by some degree of woe
We every bliss must gain;
The heart can ne'er a transport know,
That never feels a pain.

EDWARD MOORE.
1712-1757.

Fable IX. The Farmer, the Spaniel, and the Cat.

Can't I another's face commend,
And to her virtues be a friend,
But instantly your forehead lowers,
As if **her** merit lessened **yours**?

Fable X. The Spider and the Bee.

The maid who modestly conceals
Her beauties, while she hides, reveals;
Give but a glimpse, and fancy draws
Whate'er the Grecian Venus was.
But from the hoop's bewitching round,
Her very shoe has power to wound.

The Happy Marriage.

Time still, as he flies, adds increase to her truth,
And gives to her mind what he steals from her youth.

The Gamester. Act iii. Sc. 4.

'Tis now the summer of your youth: time
has not cropt the roses from your cheek,
though sorrow long has washed them.

WILLIAM SHENSTONE.
1714-1763.

Written on the Window of an Inn.

Whoe'er has traveled life's dull round,
Where'er his stages may have been,
May sigh to think he still has found
His warmest welcome at an inn.

Jemmy Dawson.

For seldom shall you hear a tale
So sad, so tender, and so true.

The Schoolmistress.

Her cap, far whiter than the driven snow,
Emblems right meet of decency does yield.

JOHN BROWN.
1715-1766.

Barbarossa. Act. v. Sc. 3.

Now let us thank the Eternal Power: convinced
That Heaven but tries our virtue by affliction,
That oft the cloud which wraps the present hour
Serves but to brighten all our future days.

DAVID GARRICK.
1716-1779.

Prologue on Quitting the Stage in 1776, 10th of June.

Their cause I plead--plead it in heart and mind;
A fellow-feeling makes one wondrous kind.

On the Death of Mr. Pelham.

Let others hail the rising sun:
I bow to that whose race is run.

THOMAS GRAY.
1716-1771.

On a Distant Prospect of Eton College.

Ah, happy hills! ah, pleasing shade!
Ah, fields beloved in vain!
Where once my careless childhood strayed,
A stranger yet to pain!
Alas! regardless of their doom,
The little victims play;
No sense have they of ills to come,
Nor care beyond to-day.
No more: where ignorance is bliss,
'Tis folly to be wise.

Progress of Poesy.

O'er her warm cheek and rising bosom move
The bloom of young Desire, and purple light of Love.

Ope the sacred source of sympathetic tears.
Thoughts that breathe, and words that burn.

The Bard.

Give ample room, and verge enough.
Youth at the prow, and Pleasure at the helm.

Elegy in a Country Churchyard.

The rude forefathers of the hamlet sleep.
The short and simple annals of the poor.
The paths of glory lead but to the grave.
Where through the long-drawn aisle and fretted vault
The pealing anthem swells the note of praise.
Hands, that the rod of empire might have swayed,
Or waked to ecstasy the living lyre.
Full many a flower is born to blush unseen,
And waste its sweetness on the desert air.
Some mute, inglorious Milton here may rest.

And read their history in a nation's eyes.
Forbade to wade through slaughter to a throne,
And shut the gates of mercy on mankind.
Along the cool, sequestered vale of life
They kept the noiseless tenor of their way.
Implores the passing tribute of a sigh.
And many a holy text around she strews,
That teach the rustic moralist to die.
Nor cast one longing, lingering look behind.
E'en from the tomb the voice of nature cries,
E'en in our ashes, live their wonted fires.

A youth, to fortune and to fame unknown.
Large was his bounty, and his soul sincere.
He gave to misery (all he had) a tear.
The bosom of his Father and his God.

Ode on the Pleasure arising from Vicissitude.

The meanest floweret of the vale,
The simplest note that swells the gale,
The common sun, the air, the skies,
To him are opening paradise.

WILLIAM COLLINS.
1720-1756.

Ode in 1746.

How sleep the brave, who sink to rest,
By all their country's wishes blessed!
By fairy hands their knell is rung;
By forms unseen their dirge is sung;
There Honor comes, a pilgrim gray,
To bless the turf that wraps their clay;
And Freedom shall awhile repair,
To dwell a weeping hermit there.

The Passions. Line 1.

When Music, heavenly maid, was young,
While yet in early Greece she sung.

Line 10.

Filled with fury, rapt, inspired.

Line 28.

'Twas sad by fits, by starts 'twas wild.

Line 60.

In notes by distance made more sweet.

Line 68.

In hollow murmurs died away.

Line 95.

O Music! sphere-descended maid,
Friend of pleasure, wisdom's aid!

Eclogue 1. Line 5.

Well may your hearts believe the truths I tell;
'Tis virtue makes the bliss, where'er we dwell.

Ode on the Death of Thomson.

In yonder grave a Druid lies.

MARK AKENSIDE.
1721-1770.

Epistle to Curio.

The man forget not, though in rags he lies,
And know the mortal through a crown's disguise.

NATHANIEL COTTON.
1721-1788.

The Fireside. St. 3.

If solid happiness we prize,
Within our breast this jewel lies;
And they are fools who roam:
The world has nothing to bestow;
From our own selves our joys must flow,
And that dear hut--our home.

St. 13.

Thus hand in hand through life we'll go;
Its checkered paths of joy and woe
With cautious steps we'll tread.

JOHN HOME.
1722-1808.

Douglas. Act i. Sc. 1.

In the first days
Of my distracting grief, I found myself
As women wish to be who love their lords.

Act ii. Sc. 1.

My name is Norval; on the Grampian hills
My father fed his flocks.

OLIVER GOLDSMITH.
1728-1774.

THE TRAVELLER.

Line 1.

Remote, unfriended, melancholy, slow.

Line 7.

Where er I roam, whatever realms to see,
My heart untravelled fondly turns to thee.

Line 22.

And learn the luxury of doing good.

Line 26.

Some fleeting good that mocks me with the view.

Line 77.

Such is the patriot's boast, where er we roam,

His first, best country ever is at home.

Line 153.

By sports like these are all his cares beguiled,
The sports of children satisfy the child.

Line 172.

But winter lingering chills the lap of May.

Line 217.

So the loud torrent, and the whirlwind's roar.
But bind him to his native mountains more.

Line 251.

Alike all ages: dames of ancient days
Have led their children through the mirthful maze;
And the gay grandsire, skilled in gestic lore,
Has frisked beneath the burden of threescore.

Line 327.

Pride in their port, defiance in their eye,
I see the lords of human kind pass by.

Line 372.

For just experience tells, in every soil,
That those that think must govern those that toil.

Line 386.

Laws grind the poor, and rich men rule the law.

Line 409.

Forced from their homes, a melancholy train.

THE DESERTED VILLAGE.

Line 14.

For talking age and whispering lovers made.

Line 51.

Ill fares the land to hastening ills a prey,
Where wealth accumulates, and men decay,
Princes and lords may flourish, or may fade,
A breath can make them, as a breath has made;
But a bold peasantry, their country's pride,
When once destroyed, can never be supplied.

Line 62.

And his best riches, ignorance of wealth.

Line 100.

A youth of labor with an age of ease.

Line 110.

While resignation gently slopes the way--
And, all his prospects brightening to the last,
His heaven commences ere the world be past!

Line 122.

And the loud laugh that spoke the vacant mind.

Line 141.

A man he was to all the country dear,
And passing rich with forty pounds a year.

Line 158.

Shouldered his crutch and showed how fields were won.

Line 161.

Careless their merits or their faults to scan,
His pity gave ere charity began.

Line 164.

And even his failings leaned to virtue's side.

Line 170.

Allured to brighter worlds, and led the way.

Line 180.

And fools who came to scoff remained to pray.

Line 184.

And plucked his gown, to share the good man's smile.

Line 192.

Eternal sunshine settles on its head.

Line 196.

The village master taught his little school.

Line 203.

Full well the busy whisper, circling round,
Conveyed the dismal tidings when he frowned.

Line 212.

For even though vanquished, he could argue still;
While words of learned length and thundering sound
Amazed the gazing rustics ranged around;
And still they gazed, and still the wonder grew
That one small head could carry all he knew.

Line 229.

Contrived a double debt to pay.

Line 254.

One native charm than all the gloss of art.

Line 264.

The heart distrusting asks, if this be joy.

Line 329.

Her modest looks the cottage might adorn,
Sweet as the primrose peeps beneath the thorn.

Line 385.

O Luxury! thou cursed by Heaven's decree.

RETALIATION.

Line 24.

Who mixed reason with pleasure and wisdom with mirth.

Line 31.

Who, born for the universe, narrowed his mind,
And to party gave up what was meant for mankind.

Line 37.

Though equal to all things, for all things unfit.

Line 94.

An abridgement of all that was pleasant in man.

VICAR OF WAKEFIELD.

Chapter viii. *The Hermit*.

Man wants but little here below,
Nor wants that little long.

Chapter xvii. *Elegy on a Mad Dog*.

The roan recovered of the bite,
The dog it was that died.

Chapter xxiv.

When lovely woman stoops to folly,
And finds too late that men betray,
What charm can soothe her melancholy?
What art can wash her guilt away?
The only art her guilt to cover,
To hide her shame from every eye,
To give repentance to her lover,
And wring his bosom, is--to die.

Elegy on Mrs. Mary Blaise.

The king himself has followed her
When she has walked before.

TOBIAS SMOLLETT.
1721-1771.

Ode to Independence.

Thy spirit, Independence, let me share;
Lord of the lion heart and eagle eye,
Thy steps I follow with my bosom bare,
Nor heed the storm that howls along the sky.

THOMAS PERCY.
1728-1811.

Reliques of English Poetry. The Baffled Knight.

He that wold not when he might,
He shall not when he wolda.

The Friar of Orders Gray.

Weep no more, lady, weep no more,
Thy sorrow is in vain;
For violets plucked the sweetest showers
Will ne'er make grow again.
Sigh no more, ladies, sigh no more,
Men were deceivers ever;

One foot on sea, and one on shore,
To one thing constant never.

From Byrd's Psalmes, Sonets, &c. 1588.

My mind to me a kingdom is;
Such perfect joy therein I find,
As far exceeds all earthly bliss
That God and Nature hath assigned.
Though much I want that most would have,
Yet still my mind forbids to crave.

BEILBY PORTEUS.
1731-1808.

Death, a Poem. Line 154.

One murder makes a villain,
Millions a hero.

JAMES BEATTIE.
1735-1766.

The Minstrel. Book i. St. 1.

Ah! who can tell how hard it is to climb
The steep where Fame's proud temple shines afar?

The Hermit. Line 8.
He thought as a sage, but he felt as a man.

Epigram. *The Bucks had dined*.

How hard their lot who neither won nor lost.

CHARLES CHURCHILL.
1741-1764.

The Rosciad. Line 861.

But spite of all the criticising elves,
Those who would make us feel--must feel themselves.

MRS. THEALE.
1740-1822.

Three Warnings.

The tree of deepest root is found
Least willing still to quit the ground;
'Twas therefore said, by ancient sages,
That love of life increased with years
So much, that in our latter stages,
When pains grow sharp, and sickness rages,
The greatest love of life appears.

WILLIAM COWPER.
1731-1800.

THE TASK.

Book i. *The Sofa*.

God made the county, and man made the town.[20]

[Note 20: "God the first garden made, and the first city Cain."--Cowley]

Book ii. *The Timepiece*.

O for a lodge in some vast wilderness,
Some boundless contiguity of shade,
Where rumor of oppression and deceit,
Of unsuccessful or successful war,
Might never roach me more.
Mountains interposed
Make enemies of nations, who had else,
Like kindred drops, been mingled into one.
England, with all thy faults, I love thee still.
Praise enough
To fill the ambition of a private man,
That Chatham's language was his mother tongue.
There is a pleasure in poetic pains
Which only poets know.
Variety's the very spice of life,
That gives it all its flavor.

Book iii. *The Garden*.

Domestic Happiness, thou only bliss
Of Paradise that hast survived the fall!

How various his employments whom the world
jails idle; and who justly in return
Esteems that busy world an idler too!

Book iv. *Winter Evening*.

And while the bubbling and loud hissing urn
Throws up a steamy column, and the cups
That cheer, but not inebriate, wait on each,

So let us welcome peaceful evening in.
'Tis pleasant, through the loopholes of retreat,
To peep at such a world; to see the stir
Of the great Babel, and not feel the crowd.

Book v. ***Winter Morn in a Walk***.

He is the freeman whom the truth makes free.

Book vi. ***Winter Walk at Noon***.

There is in souls a sympathy with sounds;
And as the mind is pitched, the ear is pleased
With melting airs, or martial, brisk or grave;
Some chord in unison with what we hear
Is touched within us, and the heart replies.
Here the heart
May give a useful lesson to the head,
And Learning wiser grow without his books.

Tirocinium.

Shine by the side of every path we tread
With such a lustre, he that runs may read.

Retirement.

Built God a church, and laughed His word to scorn.
How sweet, how passing sweet is solitude!
But grant me still a friend in my retreat,
Whom I may whisper, Solitude is sweet.

Conversation.

A fool must now and then be right, by chance.

John Gilpin.

That, though on pleasure she was bent,
She had a frugal mind.
To dash through thick and thin.
A hat not much the worse for wear

Lines to his Mother's Picture.

O that those lips had language! Life has passed
With me but roughly since I heard thee last.

Walking with God.

What peaceful hours I once enjoyed?
How sweet their memory still!
But they have left an aching void,
The world can never fill.

VERSES,
Supposed to be Written by Alexander Selkirk.

I am monarch of all I survey,
My right there is none to dispute.
O Solitude! where are the charms
That sages have seen in thy face?
But the sound of the church-going bell
Those valleys and rocks never heard,

Never sighed at the sound of a knell,
Or smiled when a Sabbath appeared.
How fleet is a glance of the mind!
Compared with the speed of its flight,
The tempest itself lags behind,
And the swift-winged arrows of light.

W. J. MICKLE.
1734-1788.

The Mariner's Wife.

His very foot has music in 't
As he comes up the stairs.

JOHN LANGHORNE.
1735-1779.

The Country Justice.

Part i

Bent o'er her babe, her eye dissolved in dew;

The big drops, mingling with the milk he drew,
Gave the sad presage of his future years,
The child of misery, baptized in tears.

DR. WALCOTT.
1738-1819.

Peter Pindar's Expostulatory Odes to a great Duke
and a little Lord. *Ode XV*.

Care to our coffin adds a nail, no doubt,
And every grin, so merry, draws one out.

MRS. BARBAULD.
1743-1825.

Warrington Academy.

Man is the noblest growth our realms supply,
And souls are ripened in our northern sky.

SIR WILLIAM JONES.
1746-1794.

A Persian Song of Hafiz.

Go boldly forth, my simple lay,
Whose accents flow with artless ease,
Like orient pearls at random strung.

Ode in Imitation of Alcoeus.

What constitutes a state?
Men who their duties know,
But know their rights, and, knowing, dare maintain.
And sovereign law, that state's collected will,
O'er thrones and globes elate,
Sits empress, crowning good, repressing ill.
Seven hours to law, to soothing slumber seven,
Ten to the world allot, and all to heaven.[21]

[Note 21: "Six hours in sleep, in law's grave study six, Four spend
in prayer, the rest on nature fix."--Sir Edward Coke.]

CAPTAIN CHARLES MORRIS.
--1832.

Billy Pitt and the Farmer.

Solid men of Boston, make no long orations;
Solid men of Boston, drink no deep potations.

JOHN TRUMBULL.
1750-1881.

McFingal. Canto i. Line 67.

But optics sharp it needs, I ween,
To see what is not to be seen.

Canto iii. Line 489.

No man e'er felt the halter draw,
With good opinion of the law.

RICHARD BRINSLEY SHERIDAN
1751-1816.

The Rivals. Act v. Sc. 3.

As headstrong as an allegory on the banks of the Nile.

The Critic. Act ii. Sc. 1.

My valor is certainly going! it is sneaking
off! I feel it oozing out as it were at the pain,
of my hands.

Act ii. Sc. 2.

Where they do agree, their unanimity is
wonderful.

School for Scandal. Act i. Sc. 1.

You shall see a beautiful quarto page, where
a neat rivulet of text shall meander through a
meadow of margin.

Act iii. Sc. 3.

Here's to the maiden of bashful fifteen;
Here's to the widow of fifty;

Here's to the flaunting, extravagant quean,
And here's to the housewife that's thrifty.
Let the toast pass;
Drink to the lass;
I'll warrant she'll prove an excuse for the glass.

The Duenna. Act i. Sc. 2.

I ne'er could any lustre see
In eyes that would not look on me;
I ne'er saw nectar on a lip
But where my own did hope to sip.

Speech in Reply to Mr. Dundas.

The Right Honorable gentleman is indebted
to his memory for his jests and to his imagination for his facts.

GEORGE CRABBE.
1754-1832.

Parish Register.

Oh! rather give me commentators plain,
Who with no deep researches vex the brain,
Who from the dark and doubtful love to run,
And hold their glimmering taper to the sun.

The Borough Schools.

Books cannot always please, however good;
Minds are not ever craving for their food.

The Borough Placers.

In this fool's paradise lie drank delight.

The Birth of Flattery.

In idle wishes fools supinely stay;
Be there a will, then wisdom finds a way.

ROBERT BURNS.
1759-1796.

Tom O'Shanter.

Where sits our sulky, sullen dame,
Gather in' her brows like gatherin' storm,
Nursin' her wrath to keep it warm.
Kings may be blest, but Tam was glorious,
O'er a' the ills o' life victorious.
But pleasures are like poppies spread,
You seize the flower, its bloom is shed;
Or like the snow falls in the river,
A moment white, then melts for ever.
As Tammie gloured, amazed and curious,

The mirth and fun grew fast and furious.

To a Mouse.

The best laid schemes o' mice an' men
Gang aft a-gley;
An' lea'e us naught but grief and pain
For promised joy.

Scots wha hae.

Let us do, or die!

Address to the Unco Guid.

Then gently scan your brother man,
Still gentler, sister woman;
Though they may gang a kennin' wrang
To step aside is human.

On Captain Grose's Peregrinations through Scotland.

If there's a hole in a' your coats,
I rede you tent it;
A chiel's amang you takin' notes,
An', faith, he'll prent it.

To a Louse.

O wad some power the giftie gie us,
To see oursel's as others see us!

It wad frae monie a blunder free us,
An' foolish notion.

Epistle to a Young Friend.

The fear o' hell 's a hangman's whip
To haud the wretch in order;
But where ye feel your honor grip,
Let that aye be your border.

The Twa Dogs.

His locked, lettered, braw brass collar
Shawed him the gentleman and scholar.

Epistle to James Smith.

O Life! how pleasant in thy morning,
Young Fancy's rays the hills adorning!
Cold, pausing Caution's lesson scorning,
We frisk away,
Like schoolboys at th' expected warning.
To joy and play.

Despondency.

O Life! them art a galling load,
Along a rough, a weary road,
To wretches such as I!

Auld Lang Syne.

Should auld acquaintance be forgot,
And never brought to min'?
Should auld acquaintance be forgot,
And days o' lang syne?

Green grow the Rashes.

Her 'prentice han' she tried on man.
And then she made the lasses, O!

Man was made to Mourn.

Man's inhumanity to man
Makes countless thousands mourn.

Death and Dr. Hornbook.

Some wee short hour ayont the twal.

Is there for honest Poverty.

The *rank* is but the guinea's *stamp*.

The man's the gowd for a' that.
A prince can mak' a belted knight,
A marquis, duke, and a that:
But an honest man's aboon his might,
Guid faith, he maunna fa' that.

The Cotter's Saturday Night.

He wales a portion with judicious care;

And "Let us worship God!" he says, with solemn air.

THOMAS MOSS.
--1808.

The Beggar.

Pity the sorrows of a poor old man,
Whose trembling limbs have borne him to your door,
Whose days are dwindled to the shortest span;
Oh! give relief, and Heaven will bless your store.

GEORGE COLMAN.
1762-1836.

BROAD GRINS.

The Maid of the Moor.

And what's impossible can't be,
And never, never comes to pass.
Three stories high, long, dull, and old,
As great lord's stories often are.

Lodgings for Single Gentlemen.

But when ill indeed,
E'en dismissing the doctor don't always succeed.

The Poor Gentleman.

Act i. Sc. 2.

Thank you, good sir, I owe you one.

Prologue to the Heir ft Law.

On their own merits modest men are dumb.

THOMAS MORTON.
1764-1836.

Speed the Plough. Act i. Sc. 1.

What will Mrs. Grundy say?

GEORGE CANNING.
1770-1827.

POETRY OF THE ANTI-JACOBIN.

The Needy Knife-Grinder.

Story! God bless you, I have none to tell, sir!
I give thee sixpence! I will see thee d--d first.

The Loves of the Triangles.

Line 178.

So down thy hill, romantic Ashbourne, glides
The Derby dilly, carrying three insides.

WILLIAM WORDSWORTH.
1770-1850.

Quilt and Sorrow.

St. 41.

And homeless near a thousand homes I stood,
And near a thousand tables pined and wanted food.

My Heart Leaps up.

The Child is father of the Man.

Lucy Gray.

St. 2.

The sweetest thing that ever grew
Beside a human door.

We are Seven.

A simple Child,
That lightly draws its breath,
And feels its life in every limb,
What should it know of death?

The Pet Lamb.

Drink, pretty creature, drink.

The Brothers.

Until a man might travel twelve stout miles,
Or reap an acre of his neighbor's corn.

Stanzas written in Thomson.

A noticeable man, with large gray eyes.

Lucy.

She dwelt among the untrodden ways
Beside the springs of Dove,
A maid whom there were none to praise,
And very few to love:
A violet by a mossy stone
Half hidden from the eye!
Fair as a star, when only one
Is shining in the sky.
She lived unknown, and few could know
When Lucy ceased to be;
But she is in her grave, and oh!
The difference to me!

The Solitary Reaper.

Some natural sorrow, loss, or pain,
That has been, and may be again.

The music in my heart I bore,
Long after it was heard no more.

Rob Hoy's Grave.

St. 9.

Because the good old rule
Sufficeth them, the simple plan,
That they should take who have the power,
And they should keep who can.

Yarrow Unvisited.

The swan on still St. Mary's Lake
Float double, swan and shadow!

Sonnets to National Independence and Liberty.

Part i. vi

Men are we, and must grieve when even the Shade
Of that which once was great is passed away.

Part i. xiv.

Thy soul was like a Star, and dwelt apart.

Part i. xvi.

We must be free or die, who speak the tongue
That Shakespeare spake; the faith and morals hold
Which Milton held.

Nutting.

One of those heavenly days that cannot die.

She was a Phantom of Delight.

A Creature not too bright or good
For human nature's daily food,
For transient sorrows, simple wiles;
Praise, blame, love, kisses, tears, and smiles.
A perfect woman, nobly planned,
To warn, to comfort, and command.

I Wandered Lonely.

That inward eye
Which is the bliss of solitude.

Ruth.

A Youth to whom was given
So much of earth, so much of heaven.

Resolution and Independence.

Part i. St. 7

I thought of Chatterton, the marvellous Boy,
The sleepless soul that perished in his pride;
Of him who walked in glory and in joy,
Following his plough, along the mountainside.

Hart-Leap Well.

Part ii

"A jolly place," said he, "in times of old!
But something ails it now: the spot is cursed."
Never to blend our pleasure or our pride
With sorrow of the meanest thing that feels.

Tintern Abbey.

Sensations sweet
Felt in the blood, and felt along the heart.
That best portion of a good man's life,
His little, nameless, unremembered acts
Of kindness and of love.
That blessed mood,
In which the burden of the mystery,
In which the heavy and the weary weight
Of all this unintelligible world,
Is lightened.
The fretful stir
Unprofitable, and the fever of the world,
Have hung upon the beatings of my heart.
The sounding cataract

Haunted me like a passion; the tall rock,
The mountain, and the deep and gloomy wood,
Their colors and their forms, were then to me
An appetite; a feeling and a love,
That had no need of a remoter charm
By thoughts supplied, nor any interest
Unborrowed from the eye.
But hearing often-times
The still, sad music of humanity.

To a Skylark.

Type of the wise who soar, but never roam;
True to the kindred points of Heaven and Home.

Peter Bell.

Prologue. St. 1.

There's something in a flying horse,
There's something in a huge balloon.

Prologue. St. 27.

The common growth of Mother Earth
Suffices me--her tears, her mirths
Her humblest mirth and tears.

Part i. St. 12.

A primrose by a river's brim
A yellow primrose was to him,
And it was nothing more.

Part i. St. 15.

The soft blue sky did never melt
Into his heart; he never felt
The witchery of the soft blue sky!

Part i. St. 26.

As if the man had fixed his face,
In many a solitary place,
Against the wind and open sky!

Miscellaneous Sonnets.

Part i. xxx.

The holy time is quiet as a Nun
Breathless with adoration.

Part i. xxxiii.

The world is too much with us; late and soon,

Getting and spending, we lay waste our powers.

Part i. xxxv.

'Tis hers to pluck the amaranthine flower
Of Faith, and round the Sufferer's temples bind
Wreaths that endure affliction's heaviest shower,
And do not shrink from sorrow's keenest wind.

Part ii. xxxvi.

Dear God! the very houses seem asleep;
And all that mighty heart is lying still!

Ecclesiastical Sonnets.

Part iii. v. ***Walton's Book of Lives***.

The feather, whence the pen
Was shaped that traced the lives of these good men,
Dropped from an Angel's wing.
Meek Walton's heavenly memory.

The Tables Turned.

Up! up! my Friend, and quit your books,
Or surely you'll grow double:
Up! up! my Friend, and clear your looks;
Why all this toil and trouble?

One impulse from a vernal wood
May teach you more of man,
Of moral evil and of good,
Than all the sages can.

A Poet's Epitaph.

St. 5.

One that would peep and botanize
Upon his mother's grave.

Personal Talk.

St. 3.

The gentle Lady married to the Moor,
And heavenly Una with her milk-white Lamb.

The Small Celandine.
(From Poems referring to the Period of Old Age.)

To be a Prodigal's Favorite--then, worse truth,
A Miser's Pensioner--behold our lot!

Elegiac Stanzas suggested by a Picture of Peele
Castle in a Storm.

St. 4.

The light that never was, on sea or land,
The consecration, and the Poet's dream.

Intimations of Immorality.

St 5.

Our birth is but a sleep and a forgetting.
But trailing clouds of glory, do we come
From God, who is our home:
Heaven lies about us in our infancy!

St. xi.

To me the meanest flower that blows can give
Thoughts that do often lie too deep for tears.

THE EXCURSION.

Book i.

The vision and the faculty divine.
The imperfect offices of prayer and praise.
The good die first,
And they whose hearts are dry as summer dust
Burn to the socket.

Book ii.

With battlements, that on their restless fronts
Bore stars.

Book iii.

Wrongs unredressed, or insults unavenged.
Monastic brotherhood, upon rock Aerial.

Book iv.

I have seen
A curious child, who dwelt upon a tract
Of inland ground, applying to his ear
The convolutions of a smooth-lipped shell;
To which, in silence hushed, his very soul
Listened intensely; and his countenance soon
Brightened with joy; for from within were heard
Murmurings, whereby the monitor expressed
Mysterious union with its native sea.
One in whom persuasion and belief
Had ripened into faith, and faith become
A passionate intuition.

Book vi.

Spires whose silent fingers point to heaven.

Book vii.

Wisdom married to immortal verse.

Book ix.

The primal duties shine aloft, like stars,
The charities, that soothe, and heal, and bless,
Are scattered at the feet of Man, like flowers.

HON. WILLIAM ROBERT SPENCER.
1770-1834.

Lines to Lady A. Hamilton.

Too late I stayed--forgive the crime;
Unheeded flew the hours.
How noiseless falls the foot of time,
That only treads on flowers!

DR. GEORGE SEWELL.
--1726.

When all the blandishments of life are gone,
The coward sneaks to death, the brave live on.

SAMUEL TAYLOR COLERIDGE.
1772-1834

The Ancient Mariner.

Part i.

And listens like a three years' child.

Part ii.

We were the first that ever burst
Into that silent sea.
As idle as a painted ship
Upon a painted ocean.
Water, water, everywhere,
Nor any drop to drink.

Part iv.

Alone, alone, all, all alone,
Alone on a wide, wide sea.

Part v.

A noise like of a hidden brook
In the leafy mouth of June.

Part vii.

He prayeth well, who loveth well
Both man and bird and beast.
He prayeth best, who loveth best
All things, both great and small.
A sadder and a wiser man,
He rose the morrow morn.

Christabel. Part ii.

Alas! they had been friends in youth;
But whispering tongues can poison truth:
And constancy lives in realms above.

The Devil's Thoughts.

And the Devil did grin, for his darling sin,
Is pride that apes humility.

Love.

All thoughts, all passions, all delights,
Whatever stirs this mortal frame,
All are but ministers of Love,
And feeds his sacred flame.

Reflections on having left a Place of Retirement.

Blest hour! it was a luxury--to be!

Hymn in the Vale of Chamouni.

Hast thou a charm to stay the morning star
In his steep course?
Risest from forth thy silent sea of pines.
Motionless torrents! silent cataracts!
Earth, with her thousand voices, praises God.

The Three Graves.

A mother is a mother still,
The holiest thing alive.

The Visit of the Gods.

Never, believe me,
Appear the Immortals,
Never alone.

The Knight's Tomb.

The Knight's bones are dust,
And his good sword rust;
His soul is with the saints, I trust.

On Taking Leave of--. 1817.
To know, to esteem, to love--and then to part,
Makes up life's tale to many a feeling heart!

Cologne.

The river Rhine, it is well known,
Doth wash your city of Cologne;
But tell me, nymphs! what power divine

Shall henceforth wash the river Rhine?

Wallenstein.

Part i. Act ii. Sc. 4.

The intelligible forms of ancient poets,
The fair humanities of old religion,
The power, the beauty, and the majesty,
That had their haunts in dale, or piny mountain,
Or forest by slow stream, or pebbly spring,
Or chasms and watery depths; all these have vanished;
They live no longer in the faith of reason.

The Death of Wallenstein.

Act. v. Sc. 1.

Clothing the palpable and familiar
With golden exhalations of the dawn.

Act v. Sc. 1.

Often do the spirits
Of great events stride on before the events.
And in to-day already walks to-morrow.

ROBERT SOUTHEY.
1774-1843.

Curse of Kehama. Canto x.

They sin who tell us love can die.
With life all other passions fly,
All others are but vanity.

CHARLES LAMB.
1775-1834.

Old Familiar Faces.

I have had playmates, 1 have had companions,
In my days of childhood, in my joyful school-days;
All, all are gone, the old familiar faces.

Detached Thoughts on Books.

Books which are no books.

THOMAS CAMPBELL.
1777-1844.

Pleasures of Hope.

Part i. Line 7.

'Tis distance lends enchantment to the view,
And robes the mountain in its azure hue.

Line 359.

O Heaven! he cried, my bleeding country save.

Line 381.

Hope for a season bade the world farewell,
And Freedom shrieked as Kosciusko fell!
O'er Prague's proud arch the fires of ruin glow,
His blood-dyed waters murmuring far below.

Part ii. Line 5.

Who hath not owned, with rapture-smitten frame,
The power of grace, the magic of a name?

Line 23.

Without the smile from partial beauty won,
Of what were man?--a world without a sun.

Line 37.

The world was sad!--the garden was a wild!
And man, the hermit, sighed--till woman smiled.

Line 45.

While Memory watches o'er the sad review
Of joys that faded like the morning dew.

Line 95.

There shall he love, when genial mom appears,
Like pensive Beauty smiling in her tears.

Line 194.

That gems the starry girdle of the year.

Line 263.

Melt, and dispel, ye spectre-doubts, that roll
Cimmerian darkness o'er the parting soul!

Line 325.

O star-eyed Science! hast thou wandered there,
To waft us home the message of despair?

Line 377.

What though my winged hours of bliss have been,
Like angel-visits, few and far between.

O'Connor's Child.

Another's sword has laid him low,
Another's and another's;
And every hand that dealt the blow,
Ah me! it was a brother's!

Lochiel's Warning.

'Tis the sunset of life gives me mystical lore,
And coming events cast their shadows before.

Ye Mariners of England.

Ye mariners of England!
That guard our native seas,
Whose flag has braved, a thousand years,
The battle and the breeze.
Britannia needs no bulwarks,

No towers along the steep;
Her march is o'er the mountain waves,
Her home is on the deep.

The Soldier's Dream.

In life's morning march, when my bosom was young.
But sorrow returned with the dawning of morn,
And the voice in my dreaming ear melted away.

Hohenlinden.

The combat deepens. On, ye brave,
Who rush to glory, or the grave!

Gertrude of Wyoming.

Part iii. St. 1.

O love! in such a wilderness as this.

WALTER SCOTT.
1771-1832.

THE LAY OF THE LAST MINSTREL.

Canto ii. St. 1.

If thou wouldst view fair Melrose aright,
Go visit it by the pale moonlight.

Canto ii. St. 12.

I was not always a man of woe.

Canto ii. St. 22.

I cannot tell how the truth may be;
I say the tale as 'twas said to me.

Canto iii. St. 2.

Love rules the court, the camp, the grove,
And men below and saints above;
For love is heaven, and heaven is love.

Canto v. St. 1.

Call it not vain; they do not err,
Who say, that, when the poet dies,
Mute Nature mourns her worshiper,
And celebrates his obsequies.

Canto v. St. 13.

True love's the gift which God has given
To man alone beneath the heaven.
It is the secret sympathy,
The silver link, the silken tie,
Which heart to heart, and mind to mind,
In body and in soul can bind.

Canto vi. St. 1.

Breathes there the man, with soul so dead,
Who never to himself hath said,
This is my own, my native land!
Whose heart hath ne'er within him burned,
As home his footsteps he hath turned
Prom wandering on a foreign strand?
Unwept, unhonored, and unsung.

Canto vi. St. 2.

O Caledonia! stern and wild,
Meet nurse for a poetic child!

Land of brown heath and shaggy wood;
Land of the mountain and the flood.

Marmion.

Canto ii. St. 27.

'Tis an old tale, and often told.

Canto v. St. 12.

With a smile on her lips and a tear in her eye.

Canto vi. St. 14.

And dar'st thou then
To beard the lion in his den?

Canto vi. St. 30,

O woman! in our hours of ease,
Uncertain, coy, and hard to please,
And variable as the shade
By the light quivering aspen made,
When pain and anguish wring the brow,
A ministering angel thou!

Canto vi. St. 32.

Charge, Chester, charge! On, Stanley, on!
Were the last words of Marmion.

Canto vi. Last Lines.

To all, to each, a fair good night,
And pleasing dreams, and slumbers light,

The Lady of the Lake.

Canto i. St. 18.

And ne'er did Grecian chisel trace
A nymph, a naiad, or a grace,
Of finer form or lovelier face.
A foot more light, a step more true,
Ne'er from the heath-flower dashed the dew.

Canto i. St. 21.

On his bold visage middle age
Had slightly pressed its signet sage.

Canto ii. St. 22.

Some feelings are to mortals given
With less of earth in them than heaven.

Canto iv. St. 1.

The rose is fairest when 'tis budding new,
And hope is brightest when it dawns from fears.

Canto iv. St. 30.

Art thou a friend to Roderick?

Canto v. St. 10.

Come one, come all! this rock shall fly
From its firm base as soon as I.
And the stern joy which warriors feel
In foemen worthy of their steel.

The Lord of the Isles.

Canto v. Stanza 18.

O many a shaft, at random sent,
Finds mark, the archer little meant!
And many a word at random spoken
May soothe, or wound, a heart that's broken!

Old Mortality.

Vol. ii. Chapter xxi.

Sound, sound the clarion, fill the fife!
To all the sensual world proclaim,
One crowded hour of glorious life
Is worth an age without a name.

Bob Roy.

Vol. i. Chapter ii.

O for the voice of that wild horn
On Fontarabian echoes borne.

The Monastery.

Vol. i. Chapter ii.

Within that awful volume lies
The mystery of mysteries!

THOMAS MOORE.
1780-1852.

Lalla Rookh. *The Fire-Worshippers*.

O, ever thus from childhood's hour
I've seen my fondest hopes decay;
I never loved a tree or flower,
But 'twas the first to fade away.

The Light of the Harem.

Alas! how light a cause may move
Dissension between hearts that love!
Hearts that the world in vain had tried,
And sorrow but more closely tied;
That stood the storm when waves were rough,
Yet in a sunny hour fall off,
Like ships that have gone down at sea,
When heaven was all tranquillity.

All that's bright must fade.

All that's bright must fade--
The brightest still the fleetest;
All that's sweet was made
But to be lost when sweetest.

Farewell! But whenever you welcome the hour.

You may break, you may shatter the vase, if you will,
But the scent of the roses will hang round it still.

REGINALD HEBER.
1783-1826.

Christman Hymn.

Brightest and best of the sons of the morning!
Dawn on our darkness, and lend us thine aid.

Missionary Hymn.

From Greenland's icy mountains,
From India's coral strand,
Where Afric's sunny fountains
Roll down their golden sand.

Palestine.

No hammers fell, no ponderous axes rung;
Like some tall palm, the mystic fabric sprung.
Majestic silence!

JONATHAN M. SEWALL.

Epilogue to Cato.

Written for the Bow Street Theatre, Portsmouth, N. H., 1778.

No pent-up Utica contracts your powers,
But the whole boundless continent is yours.

SAMUEL WOODWORTH.
1785-1842.

The old oaken bucket, the iron-bound bucket,
The moss-covered bucket, which hung in the well.

LORD BYRON.
1788-1821.

Childe Harold.

Canto i. St. 9.

Maidens, like moths, are ever caught by glare,
And Mammon wins his way where Seraphs might despair.

Canto ii. St. 2.

A schoolboy's tale, the wonder of an hour!
Dim with the mist of years, gray flits the shade of power.

Stanza 6.

The dome of Thought, the palace of the soul.

Stanza 23.

Ah! happy years! once more who would not be a boy?

Stanza 73.

Fair Greece! sad relic of departed worth!
Immortal, though no more; though fallen, great!

Stanza 76.

Hereditary bondsmen! know ye not,
Who would be free, themselves must strike the blow?

Stanza 88.

Where'er we tread, 'tis haunted, holy ground.
Age shakes Athena's towers, but spares gray Marathon.

Canto iii. St. 1.

Ada! sole daughter of my house and heart.

Stanza 21.

There was a sound of revelry by night.
And all went merry as a marriage-bell.

Stanza 28.

Battle's magnificently stern array!

Stanza 55.

The castled crag of Drachenfels
Frowns o'er the wide and winding Rhine.

Stanza 92.

The sky is changed! and such a change! O night,
And storm, and darkness! ye are wondrous strong,
Yet lovely in your strength, as is the light
Of a dark eye in woman.

Stanza 113.

I have not loved the world, nor the world me.

Canto iv. St. 1.

I stood in Venice, on the Bridge of Sighs.

Stanza 24.

The cold--the changed--perchance the dead anew,
The mourned--the loved--the lost--too many! yet how few!

Stanza 49.

Fills
The air around with beauty.

Stanza 69.

The hell of waters! where they howl and hiss.

Stanza 79.

The Niobe of nations! there she stands.

Stanza 109.

Man!
Thou pendulum betwixt a smile and tear.

Stanza 115.

The nympholepsy of some fond despair.

Stanza 145.

While stands the Coliseum, Rome shall stand
When falls the Coliseum, Rome shall fall;
And when Home falls, the world.[22]

[Note 22: The exclamation of the pilgrims in the eighth century is recorded by the Venerable Bede]

Stanza 177.

O that the desert were my dwelling-place,
With one fair spirit for my minister,
That I might all forget the human race,
And, hating no one, love but only her!

Stanza 178.

There is a pleasure in the pathless woods,
There is a rapture on the lonely shore,
There is society where none intrudes
By the deep Sea, and music in its roar.
I love not Man the less, but Nature more.

Stanza 179.

Without a grave, unknelled, uncoffined and unknown.

Stanza 185.

And what is writ, is writ.
Would it were worthier!

Memoranda from his Life.

I awoke one morning and found myself famous.

The Giaour. Line 72.

Before decay's effacing fingers
Have swept the lines where beauty lingers.

Line 92.

So coldly sweet, so deadly fair,
We start, for soul is wanting there.

Line 106.

Shrine of the mighty! can it be
That this is all remains of thee?

Line 123.

For freedom's battle, once begun,
Bequeathed by bleeding sire to son,
Though baffled oft, is ever won.

Line 418.

And lovelier things have mercy shown
To every failing but their own;

And every won a tear can claim,
Except an erring sister's shame.

Parasina. St. 1.

It is the hour when from the boughs
The nightingale's high note is heard;
It is the hour when lovers' vows
Seem sweet in every whispered word.

The Bride of Abydos.

Canto i. St. 1.

Know ye the land where the cypress and myrtle.

Stanza 6.

The light of love, the purity of grace,
The mind, the music breathing from her face,
The heart whose softness harmonized the whole
And oh! that eye was in itself a soul!

Canto ii. St. 20.

Be thou the rainbow to the storms of life!
The evening beam that smiles the clouds away,
And tints to-morrow with prophetic ray!
He makes a solitude, and calls it--peace.[23]

[Note 23: "Solitudinem fociunt--pacem appellant."
--Tacitus, Agricola, cap. 30.]

Darkness.

I had a dream which was not all a dream.

Lara.

Canto i. St. 2.

Lord of himself--that heritage of woe!

The Corsair.

Canto i. St. 1.

O'er the glad waters of the dark blue sea;
Our thoughts as boundless, and our souls as free,
Far as the breeze can bear, the billows foam,
Survey our empire, and behold our home.

Stanza 3.

She walks the waters like a thing of life,
And seems to dare the elements to strife.

Stanza 8.

The power of Thought--the magic of the Mind.
The many still must labor for the one!

Stanza 9.

There was a laughing devil in his sneer.
Hope withering fled, and Mercy sighed Farewell!

Stanza 15.

Farewell!
For in that word--that fatal word--howe'er
We promise--hope--believe--there breathes despair.

Canto iii. St. 22.

No words suffice the secret soul to show,
For truth denies all eloquence to woe.

Stanza 24.

He left a corsair's name to other times,
Linked with one virtue, and a thousand crimes.

Beppo.

Stanza 27.

For most men (till by losing rendered sager)
Will back their own opinions by a wager.

Stanza 45.

Heart on her lips, and soul within her eyes,
Soft as her clime, and sunny as her skies.

Stanza 80.

O Mirth and Innocence! O Milk and Water!
Ye happy mixtures of more happy days!

The Dream.

And both were young, and one was beautiful.
And to his eye
There was but one beloved face on earth,
And that was shining on him.
A change came o'er the spirit of my dream.
And they were canopied by the blue sky,
so cloudless, clear, and purely beautiful,
That God alone was to be seen in Heaven.

The Waltz.

Hands promiscuously applied,
Round the slight waist, or down the glowing side.

English Bards.

'Tis pleasant, sure, to see one's name in print;
A book's a book, although there's nothing in't.
As soon
Seek roses in December--ice in June.
Hope constancy in wind, or corn in chaff.
Believe a woman, or an epitaph,
Or any other thing that's false, before
You trust in critics.
Perverts the Prophets, and purloins the
Psalms.
O Amos Cottle! Phoebus! what a name!

Monody on the Death of Sheridan.

When all of Genius which can perish dies.
Folly loves the martyrdom of Fame.
Who track the steps of Glory to the grave.

Sighing that Nature formed but one such man,
And broke the die in moulding Sheridan.

Don Juan.

Canto i. St. 22.

But, O ye lords of ladies intellectual!
Inform us truly, have they not henpecked you all?

Canto i. St. 117.

Whispering I will ne'er consent, consented.

Canto xiii. St. 95.

Society is now one polished horde,
Formed of two mighty tribes, the **Bores** and **Bored**.

Canto xv. St. 13.

The devil hath not, in all his quiver's choice,
An arrow for the heart like a sweet voice.

Hebrew Melodies.

She walks in beauty, like the night
Of cloudless climes and starry skies;
And all that's best of dark and bright
Meet in her aspect and her eyes;
Thus mellowed to that tender light
Which Heaven to gaudy day denies.

CHARLES WOLFE.
1791-1823.

The Burial of Sir John Moore.

Not a drum was heard, not a funeral note,
We carved not a line, and we raised not a stone,
But we left him alone with his glory!

JOSEPH RODMAN DRAKE.
1795-1820.

The American flag.

When Freedom from her mountain height
Unfurled her standard to the air,
She tore the azure robe of night,
And set the stars of glory there.

JOHN KEATS.
1796-1820.

Endymion. Line 1.

A thing of beauty is a joy forever.

St. Agnes' Eve. Stanza 27.

Music's golden tongue
Flattered to tears this aged man and poor.

Hyperion. Line 5.

That large utterance of the early gods.

ROBERT POLLOK.
1798-1827.

The Course of Time.

Book viii. Line 616.

He was a man
Who stole the livery of the court of Heaven
To serve the devil in.

THOMAS HOOD.
1798-1845.

The Death-Bed.

We watched her breathing through the night,
Her breathing soft and low,
in her breast the wave of life
Kept heaving to and fro.
Our very hopes belied our fears,
Our fears our hopes belied;
We thought her dying when she slept,
And sleeping when she died.

The Bridge of Sighs.

One more Unfortunate
Weary of breath,
Rashly importunate,
Gone to her death.

Take her up tenderly,
Lift her with care;
Fashioned so slenderly
Young, and so fair!

SAMUEL ROGERS.

Human Life.

A guardian-angel o'er his life presiding,
Doubling his pleasures, and his cares dividing.
The soul of music slumbers in the shell,
Till waked and kindled by the master's spell;
And feeling hearts--touch them but rightly--pour
A thousand melodies unheard before!
Then, never less alone than when alone,
Those that he loved so long and sees no more,
Loved and still loves--not dead, but gone before--
He gathers round him.

A Wish.

Mine be a cot beside the hill;
A beehive's hum shall soothe my ear;
A willowy brook, that turns a mill,
With many a fall, shall linger near.

RICHARD MONCKTON MILNES.

Tragedy of the Lac de Gaube.

Stanza 2.

But on and up, where Nature's heart
Beats strong amid the hills.

The Men of Old.

Great thoughts, great feelings, came to them,
Like instincts, unawares.
A man's best things are nearest him,
Lie close about his feet.

BRYAN W. PROCTOR.

The Sea.

The sea! the sea! the open sea!
The blue, the fresh, the ever free!
I never was on the dull, tame shore,
But I loved the great sea more and more.

ALFRED TENNYSON.

Locksley Hall.

He will hold thee, when his passion shall have
spent its novel force,
Something better than his dog, a little dearer
than his horse.

I will take some savage woman, she shall rear
my dusky race.
Better fifty years of Europe than a cycle of
Cathay.

In Memoriam. xxvii.

'Tis better to have loved and lost
Than never to have loved at all.

Fatima. St. 3.

O Love, O fire! once he drew
With one long kiss my whole soul through
My lips, as sunlight drinketh dew.

The Princess. Canto iv.

Tears, idle tears, I know not what they mean,
Tears from the depth of some divine despair

Rise in the heart, and gather to the eyes,
In looking on the happy Autumn fields,
And thinking of the days that are no more.

Dear as remembered kisses after death,
And sweet as those by hopeless fancy feigned
On lips that are for others; deep as love,
Deep as first love, and wild with all regret;
O Death in Life, the days that are no more.

Canto 7.

Sweet is every sound,
Sweeter thy voice, but every sound is sweet;
Myriads of rivulets hurrying through the lawn,
The moan of doves in immemorial elms,
And murmuring of innumerable bees.
Happy he
With such a mother! faith in womankind
Beats with his blood, and trust in all things high
Comes easy to him, and though he trip and fall,
He shall not blind his soul with clay.

Lady Clara Vere de Vere.

From yon blue heaven above us bent,
The grand old gardener and his wife
Smile at the claims of loner descent.

HENRY TAYLOR

Philip Van Artevelde.

Part i. Act i. Sc. 5.

The world knows nothing of its greatest men.

EDWARD BULWER-LYTTON.

Richelieu. Act ii. Sc. 2.

Beneath the rule of men entirely great
The pen is mightier than the sword.

PHILIP JAMES BAILEY.

Festus.

We live in deeds, not years; in thoughts, not breaths;
In feelings, not in figures on a dial.
We should count time by heart-throbs. He most lives

Who thinks most, feels the noblest, acts the best.

THOMAS K. HERVEY.

The Devil's Progress.

The tomb of him who would have made
The world too glad and free.
He stood beside a cottage lone,
And listened to a lute,
One summer's eve, when the breeze was gone,
And the nightingale was mute!
Like ships, that sailed for sunny isles,
But never came to shore!

JAMES ALDRICH.

A Death-Bed.

Her suffering ended with the day,
Yet lived she at its close,
And breathed the long, long night away,
In statue-like repose!

But when the sun, in all his state,
Illumined the eastern skies,
She passed through Glory's morning gate,

And walked in Paradise.

WILLIAM CULLEN BRYANT.

Thanatopsis.

To him who in the love of Nature holds
Communion with her visible forms, she speaks
A various language.
Go forth, under the open sky, and list
To Nature's teachings.
Sustained and soothed
By an unfaltering trust, approach thy grave,
Like one that wraps the drapery of his couch.
About him, and lies down to pleasant dreams.

March.

The stormy March has come at last,
With wind and clouds and changing skies;
I hear the rushing of the blast
That through the snowy valley flies.

Autumn Woods.

But 'neath yon crimson tree,
Lover to listening maid might breathe his flame,
Nor mark, within its roseate canopy,
Her blush of maiden shame.

Forest Hymn.

The groves were God's first temples.

The Death of the Flowers.

The melancholy days are come,
The saddest of the year,
Of wailing winds, and naked woods,
And meadows brown and sear.

The Battlefield.

Truth crushed to earth shall rise again:
The eternal years of God are hers;
But Error, wounded, writhes with pain,
And dies among his worshippers.

FITZ-GREENE HALLECK.

Marco Bozzaris.

Strike--for your altars and your fires;
Strike--for the green graves of y our sires;
God, and your native land!
One of the few, the immortal names,
That were not born to die.

On the Death of Joseph Rodman Drake.

Green be the turf above thee,
Friend of my better days;
None knew thee but to love thee,
Nor named thee but to praise.

Burns.

Such graves as his are pilgrim-shrines,
Shrines to no code or creed confined--
The Delphian vales, the Palestines,
The Meccas of the mind.

CHARLES SPRAGUE.

Curiosity.

Lo, where the stage, the poor, degraded stage,
Holds its warped mirror to a gaping age.
Through life's dark road his sordid way he wends,
An incarnation of fat dividends.

Centennial Ode.

Stanza 22.

Behold! in Liberty's unclouded blaze
We lift our heads, a race of other days.

To my Cigar.

Yes, social friend, I love thee well,
In learned doctor's spite;
Thy clouds all other clouds dispel,
And lap me in delight.

HENRY W. LONGFELLOW.

A Psalm of Life.

Tell me not, in mournful numbers,
"Life is but an empty dream!"
For the soul is dead that slumbers,
And things are not what they seem.
Art is long, and Time is fleeting.
Let the dead Past bury its dead!
Lives of great men all remind us
We can make our lives sublime,
And, departing, leave behind us
Footprints on the sands of time.
Still achieving, still pursuing,
Learn to labor and to wait.

The Light of Stars.

Know how sublime a thing it is
To suffer and be strong.

It is not always May.

For Time will teach thee soon the truth,
There are no birds in last year's nest!

Maidenhood.

Standing, with reluctant feet,
Where the brook and river meet,
Womanhood and childhood fleet!

The Goblet of Life.

O suffering, sad humanity!
O ye afflicted ones, who lie
Steeped to the lips in misery,
Longing, and yet afraid to die,
Patient, though sorely tried!

Resignation.

There is no flock, however watched and tended,
But one dear lamb is there!
There is no fireside, howsoe'er defended,
But has one vacant chair.
The air is full of farewells to the dying,
And mournings for the dead.

The Golden Legend.

Time has laid his hand
Upon my heart, gently, not smiting it,

But as a harper lays his open palm
Upon his harp, to deaden its vibrations.

OLIVER WENDELL HOLMES.

A Metrical Essay.

The freeman casting with unpurchased hand
The vote that shakes the turrets of the land.
Ay, tear her tattered ensign down!
Long has it waved on high,
And many an eye has danced to see
That banner in the sky.
Nail to the mast her holy flag,
Set every threadbare sail,
And give her to the god of storms,
The lightning and the gale.

Urania.

Yes, child of suffering, thou mayst well be sure,
He who ordained the Sabbath loves the poor!--
And, when you stick on conversation's burrs,
Don't strew your pathway with those dreadful *urs*.

The Music-Grinders.

You think they are crusaders, sent

From some infernal clime,
To pluck the eyes of Sentiment,
And dock the tail of Rhyme,
To crack the voice of Melody,
And break the legs of Time.

JAMES RUSSELL LOWELL.

The Vision of Sir Launfal.

And what is so rare as a day in June?
Then, if ever, come perfect days;
Then Heaven tries the earth if it be in tune,
And over it softly her warm ear lays.

The Changeling.

This child is not mine as the first was,
I cannot sing it to rest,
I cannot lift it up fatherly
And bless it upon my breast;
Yet it lies in my little one's cradle
And sits in my little one's chair,
And the light of the heaven she's gone to
Transfigures its golden hair.

WILLIAM BASSE.
1613-1648.

On Shakespeare.

Renowned Spenser, lie a thought more nigh
To learned Chaucer, and rare Beaumont lie
A little nearer Spenser, to make room
For Shakespeare in your threefold, fourfold tomb.

DAVID EVERETT.
1769-1813.

Lines written for a School Declamation.

You'd scarce expect one of my age
To speak in public on the stage;
And if I chance to fall below
Demosthenes or Cicero,
Don't view me with a critic's eye,
But pass my imperfections by.
Large streams from little fountains flow,
Tall oaks from little acorns grow.

JOSEPH HOPKINSON.
1770-1842.

Hail Columbia.

Hail Columbia! happy land!
Hail, ye heroes! heaven-born band!

F. S. KEY.

The Star-spangled Banner.

The star-spangled banner, O long may it wave
O'er the land of the free and the home of the brave!

ALBERT G. GREENE.

Old Grimes.

Old Grimes is dead; that good old man,
We ne'er shall see him more:
He used to wear a long black coat,
All buttoned down before.

JOHN LOUIS UHLAND.

The Passage. **Translated by Mrs. Sarah Austin**.

Take, O boatman, thrice thy fee;
Take--I give it willingly;
For, invisible to thee,
Spirits twain have crossed with me.

CHRISTOPHER P. CRANCH.

Stanzas.

Thought is deeper than all speech;
Feeling deeper than all thought;
Souls to souls can never teach
What unto themselves was taught.

EATON STANNARD BARRETT.

Woman.

Not she with trait'rous kiss her Master stung,
Not she denied him with unfaithful tongue;

She, when apostles fled, could danger brave,
Last at his cross, and earliest at his grave.

MISS FANNY STEERS.

Song.

The last link is broken
That bound me to thee,
And the words thou hast spoken
Have rendered me free.

RICHARD BAXTER.
1615-1691.

Love breathing Thanks and Praise.

I preached as never sure to preach again,
And as a dying man to dying men.

ROGER L'ESTRANGE.
1616-1704.

Fables from several Authors.

Fable 398.
Though this may be play to you,
'Tis death to us.

MISCELLANEOUS.

From Apophthegms, &c., first gathered and
compiled in Latin, by Erasmus, and now
translated into English by Nicholas Vdall.
8vo. 1542. Fol. 239.

That same man, that rennith awaie,
Maie again fight an other daie.

From the Musarum Deliciae, compiled by Sir
John Mennis and Dr. James Smith. 1640

He that fights and runs away
May live to fight another day.[24]

[Note 24: See Butler--Hudibras, *ante*, p. 125.]

RICHARD GRAFTON.

Abridgement of the Chronicles of Englande. 1570. 8vo.

"A rule to knowe how many dayes euery moneth in the yeare hath."

Thirty dayes hath Nouember,
Aprill, June, and September,
February hath xxviii alone,
And all the rest have xxxi.

The Return from Parnassus. 4to. London. 1606.

Thirty days hath September,
April, June, and November,
February eight-and-twenty all alone,
And all the rest have thirty-one;
Unless that leap year doth combine,
And give to February twenty-nine.

Lines used by Joint Hall, in encourage the
Rebels in Wat Tyler's Rebellion. Hume's
History of England, Vol. I. Chap. 17.

Note i.

When Adam dolve, and Eve span,
Who was then the gentleman?

From the Garland, a Collection of Poems.

1721, by Mr. Br--st, author of a Copy of
Verses called "The British Beauties."
Praise undeserved is Satire in disguise.[25]

[Note 25: This line is quoted by Pope, in the 1st Epistle of
Horace, Book ii,--"Praise undeserved is *Scandal* in disguise."]

THOMAS A KEMPIS.
1380-1471.

Imitation of Christ.

Book i. Chapter 19.

Man proposes, but God disposes.[26]

[Note 26: This expression is of much Creator antiquity, it appears in
the Chronicle of Battel Abbey, from 1066 to 1176, page 27, Lower's
Translation, and also in Piers Ploughman's Vision, line 13994.]

Book i. Chapter 23.

And when he is out of sight, quickly also is he out of mind.

Book iii. Chapter 12.

Of two evils, the less is always to be chosen.

FRANCIS RABELAIS.
1483-1553.

Translated by Urquhart and Motteux.

Book i. Chapter 1. Note 2.

To return to our muttons.

Book i. Chapter 5.

To drink no more than a sponge.
Appetite comes with eating, says Angeston.

Book i. Chapter 11.

He looked a gift horse in the mouth.

By robbing Peter he paid Paul,...
and hoped to catch larks if ever the heavens should fall.
He did make of necessity virtue.

Book iv. Chapter 23.

I'll go his halves.

Book iv. Chapter 24.

The Devil was sick, the Devil a monk would be;
The Devil was well, the Devil a monk was he.

MIGUEL DE CERVANTES.
1547-1616.

Don Quixote. *Translated by Jarvis*.

Part i. Book iv. Ch. 20.

Every one is the son of his own works.

Part i. Book iv. Ch. 23.

I would do what I pleased, and doing what I pleased, I should have my will, and having my will, I should be contented; and when one is contented, there is no more to be desired; and when there is no more to be desired, there is an end of it.

Part ii. Book i. Ch. 4.

Every one is as God made him, and often-times a great deal worse.

Part ii. Book iv. Oh. 16.

Blessings on him who invented sleep, the mantle that covers all human thoughts.

SIR PHILIP SIDNEY.
1554-1586.

The Defense of Poesy.

He cometh unto you with a tale which holdeth children from play, and old men from the chimney-corner.
I never heard the old song of Percy and Douglass, that I found not my heart moved more than with a trumpet.

Arcadia. Book i.

There is no man suddenly either excellently good, or extremely evil.
They are never alone that are accompanied with noble thoughts.

THOMAS HOBBES.
1588-1679.

The Leviathan.

Part i. Chap. 4.

For words are wise men's counters, they do but reckon by them; but they are the money of fools.

FRANCIS BACON.
1561-1626.

Essay viii. *Of Marriage and Single Life*.

He that hath a wife and children hath given hostages to fortune, for they are impediments to great enterprises, either of virtue or mischief.

Essay 1. *Of Studies*.

Some books are to be tasted, others to be swallowed, and some few to be chewed and digested.
Reading maketh a full man, conference a ready man, and writing an exact man.

Histories make men wise, poets witty; the mathematics, subtle; natural philosophy, deep, moral, grave; logic and rhetoric, able to contend.

JOHN MILTON.
1608-1674.

Tract on Education.

In those vernal seasons of the year, when the air is calm and pleasant, it were an injury and a sullennes against Nature not to go out and see her riches, and partake in her rejoicing with heaven and earth.

The Reason of Church Government urged against Prelaty.
Introduction to Book 2.

A poet soaring in the high reason of his
fancy, with his garland and singing robes, about him.
Beholding the bright countenance of truth in the quiet and still air of delightful studies.

Areopagitica.

Methinks I see in my mind a noble and puissant nation rousing herself like a strong man after sleep, and shaking her invincible locks; methinks I see her as an eagle mewing her mighty youth, and kindling her undazzled eyes at the full midday beam.

Apology for Smectymmius.

He who would not be frustrate of his hope to write well hereafter in laudable things, ought himself to be a true poem.

THOMAS FULLER.
1608-1661.

Holy State. Book ii. Ch. 20. The Good Sea-captain.

But our captain counts the image of God, nevertheless his image cut in ebony, as if done in ivory.

Book iii. Ch. 12. Of Natural Fools.

Their heads sometimes so little, that there is no more room for wit; sometimes so long, that there is no wit for so much room.

Book iii. Ch. 22. Of Marriage.

They that marry ancient people merely in expectation to bury them, hang themselves in hope that one will come and cut the halter.

Andronicus. Ad. fin. 1.

Often the cockloft is empty, in those which
Nature hath built many stories high.

ANDREW FLETCHER OF SALTOUN.
1653-1716.

From a Letter to the Marquis of Montrose, the Earl of Rothes, &c.

I knew a very wise man that believed that, if a man were permitted to make all the ballads, he need not care who should make the laws of a nation.

HENRY ST. JOHN, VISCOUNT BOLINGBROKE.
1672-1751.

On the Study and Use of History. Letter 2.

I have read somewhere or other, in Dionysius Halicarnassus, I think, that History is Philosophy teaching by examples.

BENJAMIN FRANKLIN.
1706-1790.

Poor Richard.

God helps them that help themselves.
Dost thou love life, then do not squander
time, for that is the stuff life is made of.
Early to bed, and early to rise,
Makes a man healthy, wealthy, and wise.
Three removes are as bad as a fire.
Vessels large may venture more,
But little boats should keep near shore.
You pay too much for your whistle.

From a Letter to Miss Georgiana Shipley, on the
Loss of her American Squirrel.

Here Skugg
Lies snug,
As a bug
In a rug.

LAURENCE STERNE.
1713-1768.

Tristam Shandy.

Vol. ii. Chapter xii.

Go, poor devil, get thee gone; why should
hurt thee? This world surely is wide
enough to hold both thee and me.

Vol. iii. Chapter ix.

Great wits jump.[27]

[Note 27: "Good witts will jumpe."--Dr. Couqham, Camden Soc. Pub., p.20]

Vol. iii. Chapter xi.

Our armies swore terribly in Flanders, cried my uncle Toby--but nothing to this.

Vol. vi. Chapter viii.

And the recording angel, as he wrote it down, dropped a tear upon the word and blotted it out for ever.

SENTIMENTAL JOURNEY.

Page 1.

"They order" said I, "this matter better in France."

In the Street. *Calais*.

I pity the man who can travel from Dan to Beersheba, and cry, 'Tis all barren.

The Passport. *The Hotel at Paris*.

Disguise thyself as thou wilt, still, Slavery,
said I, still thou art a bitter draught.

Maria.

God tempers the wind to the shorn lamb.[28]

[Note 28: "Dieu mesure le vent a la brebis tondue."--Henri
Estienne. *Premices*. etc., p. 47, a collection of proverbs, published
in 1594.]

THOMAS PAINE.
1737-1809.

Letter to the Addressers.

And the final event to himself (Mr. Burke)
has been that, as he rose like a rocket, he fell
like the stick.

The Crisis. No. 1.

These are the times that try men's souls.

Age of Reason. Part ii. ad fin. (note).

The sublime and the ridiculous are so often

so nearly related that it is difficult to class
them separately. One step above the sublime
makes the ridiculous, and one step above the
ridiculous makes the sublime again.[29]

[Note 29: Probably the original of Napoleon's celebrated mot,
"Du sublime au ridicule il n'y a qu'un pas."]

DON JOSEPH PALAFOX.
1780-1843.

At the Siege of Saragossa.

War to the knife.

THOMAS B. MACAULAY.

Edinburgh Review, Oct., 1840, on Ranke's History of the Popes.

She (the Roman Catholic Church) may still exist in undiminished vigor,
when some traveller from New Zealand shall, in the midst of a vast
solitude, take his stand on a broken arch of London Bridge to sketch the
ruins of St. Paul's.

JOHN RANDOLPH.
1773-1833.

Speeches, 1828.

A wise and masterly inactivity.

WASHINGTON IRVING.

The Creole Village.

The Almighty Dollar.

FRANCIS DUC DE ROCHEFOUCAULD.
1613-1680.

Maxim ccxvii.

Hypocrisy is a sort of homage that vice
pays to virtue.

JOSEPH FOUCHE.
1763-1820.

It was worse than a crime, it was a blunder.

MISCELLANEOUS.

"The blood of the martyrs is the seed of the Church."

"Plures efficimur, quoties metimur a vobis; semen est sanguis Christianorum." *Tertullian Apologet.*, c. 50.
"Corporations have no souls."

"They (Corporations) cannot commit trespass nor be outlawed nor excommunicate, for they have no souls."--Lord Coke's Reports Part x. p. 32.
"A Rowland for an Oliver."

"These were two of the most famous in the list of Charlemagne's twelve peers; and their exploits are rendered so ridiculously and equally extravagant by the old romancers that from thence arose that saying among our plain and sensible ancestors of giving one a 'Rowland for his Oliver,' to signify the matching one incredible lie with another."--Warburton.
"It is unseasonable and unwholesome in all months that have not an R in their name to eat an oyster."--Butler's Dyet's Dry Dinner, 1599.
"Hobson's Choice."

"Tobias Hobson was the first man in England that let out hackney horses.--When a man came for a horse he was led into the stable, where there was a great choice, but he obliged him to take the horse which stood next to the stable door; so that every customer was alike well served according to his chance, from whence it became a proverb when what ought to be your election was forced upon you, to say 'Hobson's Choice.'"--Spectator, No. 509.

ADDENDA.

SHAKESPEARE.

Measure for Measure. Act v. Sc. 1.

My business in this state
Made me a looker on here in Vienna.

King Henry VI. Part i. Act i, Sc. 1.

Hung be the heavens with black

MILTON.
Sonnet xi. *To Cromwell*.

Peace hath her victories
No less renowned than war.

GEORGE HERBERT.

The Elixir.

A servant with this clause
Makes drudgery divine;
Who sweeps a room as for thy laws.
Makes that and the action fine.

SAMUEL BUTLER

Hudibras. P. ii. C. i. Line 843.

Love is a boy by poets styled;
Then spare the rod and spoil the child.

JAMES THOMSON.

Seasons. *Winter*, Line 625.

The kiss snatched hasty from the sidelong maid.

WILLIAM WORDSWORTH

Tintern Abbey.

Knowing that Nature never did betray
The heart that loved her.

INDEX

--, three poets in three distant
Agree, where they do
Air is full of farewells
Airy nothing a local habitation
--tongues
Aisle and fretted vault
Alabaster, like his grandsire cut in
All things, prove
--things to all men
--things that are, are chased
--that's bright must fade
Allegory, headstrong as an
Almanacs like actions of the last age
Almighty Dollar
Alms, when thou doest
Alone, not good that man should be
--, they are never, when with noble thoughts
Alpha and Omega
Alps on Alps arise
Altars, strike for your
Ambition, vaulting
--should be made of sterner stuff
--, to reign is worth
Angel, she drew down an
--, a guardian, she
Angel, recording
Angels unawares
--, make the, weep
--trumpet-tongued
--and ministers of grace
--face shined bright
--till our passion dies
--are painted fair to look like you

--, holy, guard thy bed
--wake thee
Angels' visits, short and
bright
--short and far between
Angel-visits, few and far between
Anger of his lip
--more in sorrow than in
Angry, be ye, and sin not
Anguish, pain is lessened by another's
--, hopeless, poured his groan
Annals of the poor
Anointed, rail on the Lord's
Answer, a soft, turneth away wrath
Anthem, pealing
Antidote, sweet oblivious
Anything, for what is worth in
Apostles fled, she when
Apostolic blows and knocks
Apothecary, civet, good
Apparel, proclaims the man
Apparitions seen and gone
Appearance, judge not by
Appetite, good digestion wait on
Appetite, cloy the hungry ed are of
--, to breakfast with what
--grown by what it fed on
Applaud these to the very echo
Apple of his eye
Appliances and means to boot
Apollo's lute, musical as
Apollos watered
Apprehension of the good

April, June, and November
Arch of London bridge
Argue, though vanquished, he could
Argues yourselves unknown
Argument, staple of his
Armor, his honest thought
Arms, take your last embrace
Arrows, Cupid kills with
Art, adorning thee with so much
--grace beyond the reach of
--, ease in writing comes from
--, than all the gloss of
--is long
Artaxerxes' throne
Arts and eloquence, mother of
Asbourne, down thy hill, romantic
Ashes to ashes
--, e'en in our
Askelon, publish it not in the streets of
Ask, and it shall be given you
Asleep, the houses seem
Ass, write me down an
Assurance double sure
Athens, the eye of Greece
Atlantean shoulders
Attempt, and not the deed, confounds
Audience, and attention drew
Audience fit, though few
Auld acquaintance
Authority, a little brief
Awake, arise, for ever fallen
Awe, in, of such a thing as I
Ax, laid to the root

Babe, bent o'er her
Babel, stir of the great
Bachelor, when I said I should die a
Backing, a plague upon such
Bacon shined, think haw
Badge of our tribe
Balances, thou art weighed in the
Ballad to his mistress' eyebrow
Ballad-mongers, one of these same meter
Ballads sung from a cart
--of a people, write the
Balloon, huge
Bank, I know a
Banner, star-spangled
Banners, hang out our
Banquet's o'er when the
Barren, 't is all
Battalions, not single, but in
Battle, mighty fallen in
--not to the strong
--and the breeze
--, perilous edge of
--, freedom's, once began
Battles, fought his, o'er again
Battle's magnificently stern array
Battlements, bore stars
Be-all, this blow might to the
Bear, like the Turk
Bears and lions grow!
Beaumont, lie a little nearer Spenser
Beauties of the North
--reveal while she hides

Beautiful, she's
--, as sweet
Beauty truly blent
--in his life
--smiling in her tears
--, fills the air around with
--, lines where, lingers
--, she walks in
--, a thing of
Beaux, where none are
Bedfellows, strange
Beer, chronicle small
Bee, how doth the little busy
Bees, innumerable
Beetle, that we tread on
Beggar, dumb, may challenge double pity
Beggary in the love
Bell, silence that dreadful
--, sullen, sounds as a
Bell, church-going
Belle, 't is vain to be a
Dells jangled, out of tune
Bent, fool me to the top of my
Bezonian? under which king
Bigness which you see
Bird of dawning
--that shunn'st the noise of folly
Birth is but a sleep
Black spirits and white
--to red began to turn
Blackberries, if reasons were as plenty as
Bladder, blows a man up like a
Blessed, more, to give

Blessings brighten as they take their flight
--on him who invented sleep
Blest, man never is, but always to be
Blind, eyes to the
Blind, if the blind lead the
Bliss gained by every woe
--, virtue makes the
--, domestic happiness, thou only
--, winged hours of
Blood, whoso sheddeth man's
--, hot and rebellious liquors in my
--, her pure and eloquent
--, felt in the
--of the martyrs
Blot, which dying he could wish to
Blow, might be the be-all
Blow, every hand that dealt the
--, themselves must strike the
Blunder, frae mony a
--, worse than a crime
Boast, the patriot's
Boatman, take thrice thy fee
Boats, little, should keep near shore
Body, absent in
--form doth fake
--, would almost say her, thought
Bond, nominated in the
--, 't is not in the
Bondman, who would he a
Bondsmen, hereditary
Bone and skin, two millers thin
Bones, full of dead men's
Bononcini, compared to

Booby, who'd give her for another
Book, that mine adversary has written a
--, your face is as a
--'s a book
Books, making of, no end
--in the running brooks
--, wiser grow without his
--cannot always please
--, quit your
--which are no
--some to be tasted
Bores and bored
Born lowly, better to be
Borrower nor lender be
Bosom, cleanse the stuffed
--'s lord sits lightly
Bosom of his Father and his God
Boston, solid men of
Botanize upon his mother's grave
Bounds of modesty
Bounty, large was his
Bourbon or Nassau
Bourne, no traveler returns
Bow, two strings to his
Bowl, mingles with my friendly
Boxes, a beggarly account of
Boy, once more who would not be a
Braggart, with, my tongue
Brain, raze out the written troubles of the
--, very coinage of your
Brains, steal away their
Brass, evil manners live in
Brave, how sleep the

--, on, ye
--, home of the
Breach, more honored in the
Bread upon the waters
Breakfast with what appetite
Breast, light within his own clear
--, eternal in the human
Breastplate, what stronger
Breath can make them
--, weary of
Breathes there the man with soul so dead
Brevity is the soul of wit
Bridge of Sighs
Briers, this working-day world is full of
Brightest and best of the sons of the morning
Britannia rules the waves
--needs no bulwarks
Britons never will be slaves
Brook, noise like a hidden
Brooks, hooks in the funning
Brotherhood, monastic
Brow, when pain and anguish wring the
Braised reed
Brutus is an honorable man
Bubbles, the earth hath
Bucket, as a drop of a
--, the old oaken
Bucks had dined
Bug, snug as a
Build, he lives to
Burden, the grasshopper a
--, bear his own
Burning, one fire burns out another's

Bush, good wine needs no
--, the thief doth tear each
Butterfly upon a wheel

Cabined, cribbed, confined
Caesar, not that I loved, less
--hath went
--, tongue in every wound of
--dead and turned to clay
Cain the first city made
Cage, nor iron bars a
Cake is dough
Cakes and ale
Caledonia, stern and wild
Calf's-skin on those recreant limbs
Calumny, thon shalt not escape
Camel, swallow a
--through the eye of a needle
Can such things be
Candle throws his beams
--out, brief
--, fit to hold a
--hold, to the sun
Canon against self-slaughter
Canopied by the blue sky
Carcass is, there will the eagles be
Card, we must speak by the
Care adds a nail to our coffin
--, knits up the ravelled sleave of
--is an enemy to life
Cares, fret thy soul with
--beguiled by sports
--dividing

Cart, now traversed the
Casca, the envious
Cassius, darest thou leap
Cast, set my life upon a
Cat in the adage
--will mew
--, endow a college or a
Cataract, the sounding
Cataracts, silent
Cathay, cycle of
Cato, big with the fate of
Caucasus, thinking on the frosty
Cause, hear me for my
Caution, cold pausing
Cave, they enter the darksome
Caviare to the general
Celestial, rosy-red
Chaff, hid in two bushels of
Chalice, the ingredients of our poisoned
Chamber where the good man meets his fate
Chance that oft decides the fate of monarchs
--to fall below Demosthenes or Cicero
Chances, most disastrous
Chaos is come again
Charge, Chester, charge
Chapel, the devil builds a
Charities that soothe
Charity shall cover the multitude of sins
Charm, no need of a remoter
Charmer, t' other dear, away
Charmers sinner it
Charybdis, your mother
Chasteneth, whom the Lord loveth, he

Chatham's language
Chatterton, marvelous boy
Chaucer, nigh to learned
Cheated, pleasure of being
Cheek, feed on her damask
--, that I might touch, that
--upon her hand
--, he that loves a rosy
Cheek, iron tears down Pluto's
--, the roses from your
Cheer, be of good
Cheese, moon made of green
Cherry, like to a double
Chickens, all my pretty
--, count your, ere they are hatched
Child, train up a
--, I spake as a
--, a wise father that knows his own
--, to have a thankless
--, a simple, that lightly draws its breath
--is father of the man
--, a curious
--, a three years
--, spoil the
Childhood, days of my
Childhood's hour
Childishness, second
Children of this world
--of light
--gathering pebbles
--of larger growth
Children's sports satisfy the child
Chin, some bee had stung

China fall
Chinks that time has made
Christ, for me to live is
Church, built God a
Church-going bell
Church, who builds to God a
Churchdoor, not so wide as a
Churchyards yawn
Cities, far from gay
City sec upon a hill
Civet, good apothecary
Clapper-clawing
Classic ground
Clay, o'er informed the tenement of
--, blind his soul with
Cloud out of the sea
--capped towers
--, overcome us like a summer's
--, sable
--but serves to brighten
Cloy the edge of appetite
Coach, go call a
Coals of fire on his head
Coat, he used to wear a long black
Coats, if there's a hole in a' your
Coil shuffled off this mortal
College, die and endow a
Cologne, wash your city of
Colossus, bestride the world like a
Column, throws up a steamy
Combat deepens
Combination and a form indeed
Come live with me

Come what come may
Comforters, miserable
Coming events
Commentators, each dark passage shun
--, plain
Communion sweet, quaff
Companions, I have had
Comparisons are odorous
--are odious
Compass, a narrow
Compulsion, give you a reason on
Concealment, like a worm in the bud
Conceals, the maid who modestly
Conceits, be not wise in your own
Conclusion, most lame and impotent
--, denoted a foregone
Concord of sweet sounds
Confirmations strong
Conflict, dire was the noise of
Conclusion, worse confounded
Congregate, merchants most do
Conjectures. I am weary of
Conquer love, they, that run away
Conquerors, a lean fellow beats all
Conscience with injustice is corrupted
--makes cowards of us all
--of her worth
Consideration, like an angel
Constable, outrun the
Consummation devoutly to be wished
Contemplation he, and valor, formed
Content, humble livers in
--, farewell

Contentment, the noblest mind, has
Contradiction, woman's a
Cord be loosed
Corn, reap an acre of
Corporations, no souls
Corsair's name, he left a
Cottage, the soul's dark
Cottage, stood beside a
Counsels, perplex and dash maturest
Counselors, safety in the multitude of
Country, undiscovered
--, God made the
Courage, screw your, to the sticking place
--mounteth with occasion
Course, I have finished my
--of true love never did run smooth
Course of empire
Courtesy, I am the very pink of
Counterfeit presentment
Coward, thou slave
--upon instinct
Cowards die many times
--, what can ennoble
Crabtree, and old iron rang
Creator, remember thy
Creature not too bright
Credulity, ye who listen with
Crime, within thee, undivulged
--, it was worse than a
Critics, not trust in
Critical, nothing if not
Criticising elves
Cross, sparkling, she wore

--, last at his
Crotchets in thy head now
Crown of glory
Crown, uneasy lies the head that wears a
Cruel as death
Crumbs, dogs eat of the
Crutch, shouldered his
Cry is still they come
--and no wool
Cunning, let my right hand forget her
Cupid kills with arrows
--is painted blind
Cups, freshly remembered in their flowing
--that cheer but not inebriate
Current of a woman's will
Curses, rigged with, dark
--, not loud, but deep
Custom stale her infinite variety
Cut, the most unkindest
Cycle and epicycle
Cynosure of neighboring eyes
Cypress and myrtle
Cytherea's breath

Daffodils that come before the swallow
Dagger I see before me
Daggers-drawing
Dale, haunts in
Dame, our sulky sullen
Dames, of ancient days
Damn with faint praise
Damnation, the deep, of his taking off
Damned to everlasting fame

Dan to Beersheba
Dance, when you do
--attendance
Daniel come to judgment
Dare, what man dare, I
Dark, illumine what is
Darkly, through a glass
Darkness visible
Dart, like the poisoning of a
Daughter, still harping on my
David, Nathan said to
Dawn, exhalations of the
Day, what a, may bring forth
--, sufficient unto the
--, jocund, stands tiptoe
--, as it tell upon a
--, brought back my night
--. the great, important
--, her suffering ended with the
Days, one of those heavenly
--, race of other
--, the melancholy
Dead and turned to clay
--past bury its
Death, they were not divided in
--in the pot
Death in the midst of life
--, where is thy sting
--, be thou faithful unto
--most in apprehension
--, the way to dusty
--, the valiant lasts but once
--grinned horrible

--, soul under the ribs of
--loves a shining mark
--nature never made
--, cruel as
Death, a simple child know of
--, cowards sneak to
--to us, play to you
Death's pale flag
Debt, a double, to pay
Decay, seen my fondest hopes
Decay's effacing fingers
December, seek roses in
Decencies, those thousand
--daily flow from
Decency, want of, want of sense
--, emblems right meet of
Deed, so shines a good
--without a name
Deeds, ill done
--, we live in
Deep, vasty, spirits from the
--yet clear
--, in the lowest, a lower
Deer, let the strucken, go weep
Defence, immodest words admit of no
Defer, 'tis madness to
Degrees, fine by
Deliberation sat and public care
Delight to pass away the time
--in this fool's paradise
Delightful task
Democraty, wielded at will that fierce
Den, beard the lion in his

Denied, lie comes too near who comes to be
Denmark, something rotten in
Depart, loth to
Derby dilly
Descent, claims of long
Description, beggared all
Desire, kindled soft
--bloom of young
Despair, love can hope where reason would
--, shall I wasting in
--, depth of some divine
Despond, slough of
Destruction, pride goeth before
Devil can cite Scripture
--, give the, his due
--. tell the truth and shame the
--, resist the
--take the hin'most
--was sick
--a monk was he
--, go, poor
Dew, thaw and resolve itself into a
Dewdrop from the lion's mane
Dial to the sun
Dial, figures on a
Die, ay, but to
--, stand the hazard of the
--because a woman's fair
--, taught us how to
--let us do or
--, heavenly days that cannot
--, who tell us love can
--, broke the, in moulding Sheridan

Digestion wait on appetite
Dignity and love, in every gesture
Dine, wretches hang that jurymen may
Dined, the bucks had
Dinner of herbs, better is
Dire was the noise of conflict
Discontent, the winter of our
--, waste long nights in pensive
Discretion the better part of valor
Disguise thyself as thou wilt
Distance lends enchantment
Distressed, griefs that harass the
Dividends, incarnation of fat
Divine, to forgive
Divinity in odd numbers
Divinity doth hedge a king
--that shapes our ends
--that stirs within us
Doctor, dismissing the
Doctors disagree, who shall decide when
Doctrine, orthodox
Dog, living, better than dead lion
--, let no, bark
--, not one to throw at a
--, and bay the moon
--will have his day
--it was that died
--, something better than his
Dogs eat of the crumbs
--throw physic to the
--, the little, and all
Dogs delight to bark and bite
Done quickly

Doom, stretch out to the crack of
--, regardless of their
Door, sweetest thing beside
Dorian mood of flutes
Dove, that I had wings like a
Doves, harmless as
Dread of something after death
Dream, consecration and the poets
--, a change came o'er the spirit of my
--, life is but an empty
Dreams, we are such stuff as
--, so full of fearful
Drink, if he thirst, give him
--to me only
--deep, or taste not
--, pretty creature
Driveller and a show
Druid lies in yonder grave
Drum, not a, was heard
Drunken man, stagger like a
Dues, render unto all their
Dumb on their own merits
Duncan hath borne his faculties
--is in his grave
--, thou art
--shalt thou return unto
--, his enemies shall lick the
Duncan's return to the earth
Dust to dust
--, smell sweet and blossom in the
--, hearts dry as summer's
--, the knight's bones are
Duty, perceive here a divided

Duties, primal, shine aloft
Dying man to dying men

Eagle mewing her mighty youth
Eagles gather where the carcass is
Eagle's fate and thine are one
Ear, word of promise to the
--, give very man thy
--, more is meant than meets the
--, wrong sow by the
Earliest at his grave
Early to lied
Ears, let him hear that hath
--, in my ancient
Earth to earth
--, put a girdle round the
--, thou sure and firm-set
--, more things in heaven and
--, so much of
--, the common growth of mother
--, but one beloved face on
--, truth crushed to
Earthy, of the earth
Ease in mine inn
--and alternate labor
Eat, drink, and be merry
Eaten me out of house and home
Echo, applaud thee to the very
Eclipse, built in the
Education forms the mind
Either, happy could I be with
Elegant sufficiency
Elephants, place for want of towns

Elements so mixed in him
Elms, immemorial
Eloquent, old man
Elysium, lap in it
Employments, how various his
Enchantment, distance lends
Endure, when pity, then, embrace
Endured, not to be
Enemies, his, shall lick the dust
--, naked to mine
Enemy, feed thine
Engineer, hoist with his own petard
England, with all thy faults, I love thee still
Enterprises, impediments to great
Envy withers at another's joy
Epitaph, believe a woman or an
Epitome, all mankind's
Err, to, is human
Error writhes with pain
Errors like straws upon the surface
Eruption, bodes some strange
Estate, fallen from his high
Eternal sunshine
Eternity to man
Ethiopian, can the, change his skin
Eve, from noon to dewy
Evening, welcome peaceful
--, now came still
Events, coming
--, spirits of great
Ever charming, ever new
Everything by starts
Evidence of things not seen

Evil, sufficient unto the day is the
--, be not overcome of
--communications corrupt good manners
--report and good report
--, money is the root of all
--that men do lives after them
--be thou my good
--, still educing good
Evils, chose the least of two
Excel, 't is useless to
Excess, wasteful and ridiculous
Expectation, better bettered
Experience to make me sad
Extremes in nature
Eye for eye
Eye, let every, negotiate for itself
--in a fine frenzy rolling
--, looking on it with lack-luster
--, white wench's black
--, more peril in thine
--sublime declared absolute rule
--, heaven in her
Eyebrow, ballad made to his mistress'
Eyes to the blind
--, no speculation in those
--, look your last
--, drink to me only with thine
--, rapt soul sitting in thine
--, not a friend to close his
--, history in a nation's
--the glowworm lend thee
--, a man with large gray
--, soul within her

Face, the mind's construction in the
--, visit her too roughly
--, human, divine
--, no tenth transmitter of a foolish
--, can't I another's, commend
--, music breathing from her
--in many a solitary place
--, finer form or lovelier
Faces, the old familiar
Facts, indebted to his imagination for his
Faculties, so meek, bath borne his
Faculty divine
Fade, all that's bright must
Failings leaned to virtue's side
Fair, is she not passing
--is foul
--, none but the brave deserve the
Faith, we walk by
--, remember your work or
--, I have kept the
--is the substance of
--, no tricks in plain and simple
--, his, perhaps might be wrong
--, for modes of
--and morals, Milton held
--, amaranthine flower of
--, belief had ripened into
Falcon, towering in her pride
Fall, O what a, was there
Failing-off was there
Fame is the spur
--, damned to everlasting

--, hard to climb the steep of
--, the martrydom of
Fame's proud temple
Famous by my pen
--, awoke and found myself
Fancies, troubled with thick-coming
Fancy, chewing the food of 'sweet and bitter
Fancy's rays the hills adorning
Fashion passeth away
--, glass of
Fast and furious
Fat, let me have men that are
Fate, take a bond of
--, roll darkling down the torrent of
Father, no more like my
Faults, be blind to her, a little blind
--, with all the, I love thee still
Favorite, to be a prodigal's
Fawning, thrift may follow
Fear, perfect love casteth out
--, with hope, farewell
Fearfully and wonderfully made
Fears, saucy doubts and
--, our hopes belied our
Feast, bare imagination of a
--of nectared sweets
--of reason
Feather, of his own, espied a
--, a wit 's a
--, to waft a
Feature, cheated of
Feel, would make us, must feel themselves
Feelings, great, came to them

Feels, meanest thing that
Feet beneath her petticoat
--like snails did creep
Feet, standing with, reluctant
Felicity, we make or find our own
Fell, I do not like thee, Doctor
Fellow that had losses
--of infinite jest
Fellow-feeling makes us kind
Female errors fall
Fever, after life's fitful
Few are chosen
Field be lost, what though the
Fields, 'a babbled of green
Fiery soul working out its way
Fife, ear-piercing
Fight, I have fought a good
Fights and runs away, he that
Fine, by degrees
--by defect
Finger, slow unmoving
Fire, while was musing, the
--, great a matter kindled by a little
--, one, burns out another's
--, pale his uneffectual
--, three removes as bad as a
Fires, their wonted
Firmament, the spacious
Fit audience find, though few
Fit'-, 'twas said by
Flame, adding fuel to the
Flanders, our armies swore terribly in
Flesh, all, is grass

--is weak

--, O that this too, too solid

--is heir to

--and blood can't bear it

Flint, wear out the everlasting

Flood, taken at the

Flow of soul

Flower, full many a

Floweret of the vale

Flowre, or herbe, no daintie

Fly, to drown a

Foe, unrelenting, to love

Foemen worthy of their steel

Foes, thrice he routed all his

Folly as it flies

--grow romantic

--, when woman stoops to

Food, minds not ever craving for

--, pined and wanted

--, nature's daily

Fool to make me merry

--, at thirty man suspects himself a

--must now and then be right

Fools, yesterdays have lighted

--, suckle

--rush in where angels fear to tread

--they are who roam

--who came to scoff

--, paradise of

Fools, in idle wishes

Foot, O, so light a

Forefathers of the hamlet sleep

Forever fortune wilt thou prove

Forget! illness, steep my senses in
Forgive, to, is divine
Form, mould of
Fortune, railed on lady
--, leads on to
Fortune's power, I am not now in
Forty pounds a year, rich with
Foxes have holes
Fragments, gather up the
Frailty, thy name is woman
France, they order this better in
Free, who would be
Freedom from her mountain height
--shrieked when Kosciusko tell
Freedom's battle once begun
Freeman, whom the truth makes free
Free-will, foreknowledge absolute
Friend, a handsome house to lodge a
--, knolling a departing
Friends, call you that backing of your
--thou hast and their adoption tried
Friendship constant, save in love affairs
Front, his fair large
Frosty but kindly
Fruit, known by his
--, the ripest first falls
Fuel to the flame
Full, without o'erflowing
Funeral baked meats
Furious, fun grew fast and
Furnace, sighing like
Fury, full of bouce and
--with the abhorred shears

--, filled with

Gain, to die is
Gale, simplest note that swells the
Gall enough in thy ink
Galligaskins, have long withstood
Garland and singing robes
Gath, tell it not in
Gather ye rosebuds
Gay, and innocent as
Genius, when all of which can perish, dies
Gentle yet not dull
Geographers, in Afric maps
Gentleman and scholar
--, where was then the
Gentlemen who write with ease
Ghost, there needs no
--, like an ill-used
Giant dies
Giant's strength, excellent to have a
Gibes, where be your
Giftie gie us, O wad some power the
Gilead, is there no balm in
Girdle round about the earth
Glare, maidens are caught by
Glass darkly, through a
--, he was indeed the
Glory, the paths of
--, trailing clouds of
--, who track the steps of
--, rush to
Glory's morning gate
Glove, O that I were a

Glowworm, her eyes the, lend thee
Glowworms uneffectual fire
Gnat, strain at a
Go and do thou
Go, Soul, the body's guest
Go his halves
God and mammon
--hath joined together
--, had I but served my
--the first garden made
--, just are the ways of
--, the noblest work of
--save the king
--the Father, God the Son
--made the country
--helps them that helps themselves
--tempers the wind
Going, stand not upon the order of your
Gold, all that glisters is not
--, gild refined
Good for us to be here
--, all things work together for
Good, hold fast that which is
--men and true
--in everything
--, men do, is oft interred with their bones
--the more communicated
--the gods provide thee
--by stealth
--, luxury of doing
--, some fleeting
--die first
Good-night, to all, to each

Goose-pen, though thou write with a
Grace, the melody of every
--was in all her steps
--beyond the reach of art
--, the power of
--, purity of
Grandsire frisked
Grapes, have eaten sour
Grasshopper shall be a burden
Gratulations flow in streams unbounded
Grave, with sorrow to the
--, where is thy victory
--to gay
--, hungry as the
--, glory leads but to the
--, Lucy is in her
--, glory or the
Graves, find ourselves dishonorable
--stood tenantless
Great, none think the, unhappy
Greatness, some achieve, etc.
--, a long farewell to all my
Greece, and fulmined over
Grecian chisel trace
Greek, it was, to me
--as naturally as pigs squeak
Greeks, when Greeks joined
Grew together, like a double cherry
Gray hairs with sorrow to the grave
Grief, patience smiling at
--, every one can master a
--, a plague of sighing and
--, perked up in a glistering

--, of my distracting
Griefs, some, are med'cinable
--that harass the distressed
Groan, hopeless anguish, poured his
Groans, mine old, ring yet
Groves were God's first temples
Ground, on classic
Grundy, what will Mrs., say
Gudgeons, ere they're catched
Guest, the going
--, speed the parting
Guides, blind

Habit, costly thy
Habitation, a local
Hail, holy light
--, wedded love
Hair to stand on end
--, distinguish and divide a
Hal, no more of that
Halter, now fitted the
--draw, no man e'er felt the
Hand, against every man
--, cloud like a man's
--findeth to do, do it
--, thy left, know, etc.
--, with an unlineal
--open as day
--, leans her cheek upon her
--which beckons me
--in hand through life
Handel's but a ninny
Handle not, taste not

--, off with his
--, plays round the
--, his small
--, a useless lesson to the
Heads, hide their diminished
Hearse, underneath this sable
Heart, man after his own
--, hope deferred maketh the, sick
--knoweth his own bitterness
--, out of the abundance of
--, be not troubled
--, merry, goes all the day
--, untainted
Heart, ruddy drops of my sad
--, not more native to the
--, conies not to the
--a transport know
--untraveled turns to thee
--distrusting asks if this be joy
--, music in my
--, felt along the
--, never melt into his
--, tale to many a feeling
--on her lips
--, an arrow for the
--, on and up where nature's
Hearts, ay in my heart of
--, of all that human, endure
--pour a thousand melodies
Heaven, droppeth as the gentle rain from
--, winds of
--of hell
--, better to reign in hell than serve in

--, hell I suffer seems a
--in her eye
--, quite in the verge of
--tries our virtues by affliction
--commences ere the world be past
--, so much of
--and home, kindred points of
--, spires point to
--God alone was to be seen in
Heaven's hand, argue not against
Heavens, hung be the
Hecuba to him
Heed, take, lest be fall
Height of this great argument
Heir to, that flesh is
Hell it is in suing long to bide
--no fury like a woman scorned
Hercules, than I to
Hermit, man the
Hero perish or sparrow fall
Herod, cat-herods
High, to soar so
--life furnishes high characters
Hill, a cot beside the
Hills peep o'er bills
--, o'er the, and far away
--, heart beats strong amid the
Hinges, pregnant, of the knee
Hint, upon this, I spake
Hip, I have thee on the
History or by tale
--, this strange, eventful
--read in a nation's eyes

--is philosophy teaching by examples
Hit, a very palpable
Hitherto shalt thou come
Hobson's choice
Hole, might stop a
Hold a candle
Holy text she strews
Homage that vice pays to virtue
Home, man goeth to his long
Home, eaten me out of house and
--, best country ever is at
Homer, read, once
Homes, homeless near a thousand
Honest man's the noblest work
Honesty, armed so strong in
Honor, prophet not without
--, to pluck right
--, loved I not, more
--but an empty bubble
--, the post, of, is a private station
--and shame from no condition rise
--grip, feel your
Honor's lodged, place where
Honors thick upon him
Hoop's bewitching round
Hope deferred
--, no other medicine but
--, true, is swift
--, tender leaves of
--never comes that come to all
--, farewell
--springs eternal
--, while there's life there's

Hush, my dear, lie still and slumber
Hyacinthine locks
Hyperion to a satyr
--curls
Hypocrisy is the homage vice pays to virtue

"I dare not" wait upon "I would,"
I owe you one
I would do what I pleased
Ice, to smooth the
--, be thou chaste as
Idea, teach the young
Idiot, tale told by an
Idler, busy world an
If is the only peacemaker
If all the world and love were young
Ignorance, let me not burst in
--is bliss
--of wealth
Ill wind turns none to good
Ills, bear those, we have
--the scholar's life assail
--, a prey to hastening
Image of God in ebony
Imagination bodies forth
--, to sweeten my
--boast hues like mature
--for his facts
Imaginings, present fears less than horrible
Immodest words admit of no defence
Immortal, grow, as they quote
Immortality, quaff
--, this longing after

Immortals never appear alone
Imparadised in one another's arms
Impediment, marched on without
Impediments to great enterprises
Imperfections on my head
Impossible can't be
Inactivity, masterly
Increase of appetite
Independence let me share
Indian, lo the poor
Infancy, heaven lies about us in
Infirmities, a friend should bear a friend's
Ingratitude, unkind as man's
Inn, take mine ease in mine
--, warmest welcome at an
Innocence, and mirth
Insides, carrying three
Insubstantial pageant
Instincts unawares
Insults unavenged
Iron entered into his soul
--, rule thee with a rod of
--, the man that meddles with cold
Isles, ships that sailed for sunny
Jade, let the galled, wince
Jail, the patron and the
Jealousy, it is the green-eyed monster
Jerusalem, if I forget thee
Jest, put his whole wit in a
Jest, the most bitter is a scornful
Jests, indebted to his memory for his
Jew, hath not a, eyes
--, I thank thee

Jewel, a precious, in his head
Jews might kiss and infidels adore
John, print it, some said
Joint, the time is out of
Jove laughs at lover's perjuries
Joy, the oil of
--, glides the smooth current o' domestic
--, forever, a thing of beauty is a
Joys, fading, we dote upon
--must flow from ourselves
Judean, like the base
Judges soon the sentence sign
Judgments as our watches
Julius, ere the mightiest, fell
June, leafy month of
--, seek ice in
Juno's eyes, sweeter than the lids of
Jurymen may dine
Justice, this even-handed

Keeper, am I my brother's
Kick where honor's lodged
Kid, the leopard lie down with the
Kin, makes the whole world
Kin, a little more than
Kind, fellow-feeling makes one wondrous
Kindness, too full of the milk of human
King, every inch a
--, catch the conscience of the
--, here lies our sovereign lord, the
--himself has followed her
Kingdom, my mind to me a
Kings it makes gods

Kiss, one kind, before we part
--, my whole soul through a
--snatched hasty
Kisses after death remembered
Kitten, and cry mew
Knave, how absolute the, is
Knaves, untaught, unmannerly
Knee, crook the hinges of the
Knell that summons thee
--, the shroud, etc.
--rung by fairy hands
Knew, carry all he
Knife, war to the
Knight, a prince can mak' a belted
Knock and it shall be opened
Know then thyself
Known, to be forever
Kosoiusko fell

Labor of love
--, we delight in
Labor, ease and alternate
Laborer worthy of his reward
Laborers are few
Ladies be but young and fair
--, intellectual
Lady doth protest too much
Lady's in the case
Lamb to the slaughter
--of God, behold the
--, Una with her milk white
Land, far into the bowels of the
--, light that never was on

--, my own, my native
--of brown heath
--, know ye the
--of the free
Landscape tire the view
Language-nature's end of
--, that those lips had
Large streams from little fountains flow
Lark at heaven's gate sings
Lasses, then she made the
Last, not least, in love
--at his cross
--link is broken
Late, known too
Laugh, the world and its dread
--that spoke the vacant mind
Law, love is the fulfilling of the
--, rich men rule the
--, seven hours to
Law, sovereign, sits empress
Laws grind the poor
Laws in-lungs call cause or cure
Lay, go forth my simple
Leaf, lade as a
--, the sear, the yellow
Leap, look before you ere you
Learning, whence is thy
--, a little is a dangerous thing
Leather or prunella
Leaven leavenet the whole lump
Leer, assent with civil
Legion, my name is
Leopard, his spots

Less, beautifully
--, of two evils choose the
Let dearly or let alone
--others hail
Libertine, the air a chartered
Liberty, I must have, withal
Lief not be, as live to be
Life, death in the midst of
--, the crown of
--, care's an enemy to
--, nothing became him like the leaving of his
--, I bear a charmed
--in short measures, may perfect be
--, slits the thin spun
--, while there is, hope
--'s a jest
--, protracted, is protracted woe
--'s dull round
Life, love of, increased with years
--, variety 's the spice of
--, how pleasant is thy morning
--, thou art a galling load
--, best portion of a good man's
--, blandishments of, are gone
--, one crowded hour of
--, like a thing of
--, the wave of
--is but an empty dream
Light, walk while ye have
--, a burning and a shining
--, casting a dim, religious
--, swift-winged arrows of
Lights, burning

--that mislead the morn
--of mild philosophy
Lilies of the field, consider the
Lily, to paint the
Line upon line
--, we carved not a
Lines fallen in pleasant places
Lion in the way
--, living dog better than a dead
--, the devil as a roaring
--, beard the
Lion-heart, lord of the
Lion's hide, thou wear a
--inane, dewdrop from the
Lip, coral, admires
--, I ne'er saw nectar on a
Lips, when I ope my
--were red
--, smile on her
--, heart on her
--, O that thou had language
Liquors, hot and rebellions
Lisped in numbers
Live, taught us how to
--while you live
--to please, must please to live
Lively to severe
Livery of heaven
Lives, lovely and pleasant in their
Lobster, boiled like, a
Local habitation and a name
Locks, never shake thy gory
Lodge in some vast wilderness

Loins be girded
Look, a lean and hungry
--before you leap
--, longing, lingering
Looker-on here in Vienna
Looks, the cottage might adorn
Lord hath taken away
--, bosom's, sits lightly
--of himself though not of lands
--Fanny spins a thousand such a day
Lords, wish to be who love their
--of human kind
Lords, stories of great
Losses, fellow that had
Lost, who neither won nor
Lothario, is this that gallant, gay
Lot's wife, remember
Love to me was wonderful
--, greater, hath no man
--, labor of
--casteth out fear
--, she never told her
--sought is good
--looks not with the eyes
--never did run smooth
--, last not least in
--, beggarly in
--prove variable
--, ecstasy of
--, live with me, and be my
--'s proper hue
--in every gesture
--, pity's akin to

--and hate in like extreme
--, an unrelenting foe to
--, purple light of
--of Life increased with years
--, all ministers of
--in such a wilderness
--is heaven
--, true, is the gift of Heaven
--rules the court
--, deep as first
--is a boy
Loved not wisely
--and lost, better to have
Loveliness needs no ornament
Lover, why so pale
Lover's perjuries
Lower, he that is down can fall no
Lucifer, falls like
Lucre, not greedy of filthy
Luster, I ne'er could any, see
Lute, listened to a
Luxury of doing good
--cursed by heaven s decree
--to be
Lydian airs, lap me in
Lying, this world is given to
Lyre waked to ecstasy

Macduff, lay on
Mad, that he is, 'tis true
--, pleasure in being
--, an undevout astronomer is
Madness, tho' this be, yet there 's method in it

--, great wits allied to
--to defer
Magic numbers
Maid who modestly conceals
--none to love and praise
Maiden meditation
--of bashful fifteen
--shame, blush of
Maidens are caught by glare
Malice, nor set down aught in
Mammon, ye cannot serve God and
Man should not be alone
--is born unto trouble
Man, mark the perfect
--, stagger like a drunken
--under his fig-tree
--shall not live by bread alone
--, profited, for what is
--lay down his life
--, be born again
--soweth, that shall he reap
--shall bear his own burden
--, proud man
--, a proper, as any one shall see
--that hath no music
--dare do all that may become a
--dare, I dare
--, could have better spared a better
--so faint, so spiritless
--, this is the state of
--that hangs on princes' favors
--of such a feeble temper
--, this was a

--'s as true as steel
--take him for all in all
--, what a piece of work is
--delights not me
--that is not passion's slave
--, give the world assurance of a
--, wished Heaven had made her such a
--, old, eloquent
--that meddles with cold iron
Man, beware the fury of a patient
--, as tree as nature first made
--, happy the, and happy lie alone
--, expatiate free o'er all this scene of
--never is, but always to be blest
--, the proper study of mankind is
--virtuous and vicious must be
--, worth makes the
--, honest, the noblest work of God
--of Ross
--, where the good, meets his fate
--of wisdom is the man of years
--wants but little
--makes a death nature never made
--, all may do what has been done by
--that blushes is not quite a brute
--, little round, fat, oily
--forget not, though in rags he lies
--to all the county dear
--, abridgment of all that was pleasant in
--recovered of the bite
--, be felt as a
--is the noblest growth our realms supply
--, gently scan your brother

--, her 'prentice han' she tried on
--'s inhumanity to man
Man's the gowd for a' that
--, pity the sorrows of a poor old
--, child is father of the
--, teach you more of
--prayeth well and best
--, a sadder and a wiser
--of woe, I was not always
--with soul so dead
--, I love not, the less
--'s best things
--proposes, God disposes
--, no, suddenly good
--, full, made by reading
Mankind, wisest, brightest, meanest of
--, survey, from China to Peru
Manna, his tongue dropped
Manners, evil communications corrupt good
Mansions, many, in my Father's house
Many are called
Mar what's well
March, beware the Ides of
--, in life's morning
--, the stormy, has come
Mare, gray, the better horse
Margin, a meadow of
Mariners of England
Mark, death loves a shining
--, the archer little meant
Marmion, the last words of
Marriage bell, merry as a
--tables, coldly furnish forth the

Married, I did not think to live till I were
Marrying ancient people
Mars, an eye like
Martyrs, blood of the
Mary hath chosen that good part
Mast, nail to the
Mattock and the grave
May, chills the lap of
Maze, a mighty
Meaner beauties of the night
Medes and Persians, law of the
Medicine, miserable have no other
Meditation, fancy free
Melancholy, green and yellow
--, most musical
Melodies, a thousand
Melody, crack the voice of
Melrose, if thou wouldst view
Memory, Walton's heavenly
--, begin to throng into my,
Men, are you good and true
--have died
--, in the catalogue ye go for
--'s evil manners live in brass
--, sleek-headed
--, tide in the affairs of
Men made by nature's journeymen
--, justify the ways of God to
--, busy hum of
--are but children
--, impious, bear sway
--, some to business take
--think all men mortal

--talk only to conceal their mind
--, rich, rule the law
--were deceivers ever
--who their duties know
--, schemes of mice and
--by losing rendered sager
--, world knows nothing of its greatest
--, beneath the rule of
--, lives of great, remind us
Merchants most do congregate
Mercy and truth are met
--is not strained
--, temper justice with
--, shut the gates of
Merit, as if her, lessened yours
--, modest men dumb on their own
Mermaid, things done at the
Merriment, flashes of
Merry when I hear sweet music
Metal more attractive
--, sonorous
Metaphysic wit, high as
Mettle, grasp it like a man of
Mice, like little, stole in and out
--, best laid schemes of
Midnight dances
--oil consumed
Mien, vice is a monster of so frightful
Might, he that would not when he
Mighty, how are the, fallen
Miles, might travel, twelve stout
Milk of human kindness
--and water, O

Mill, brook that turns a
Millions of spiritual creatures
Millstone hanged about his neck
Milton, some mute, inglorious
Mind, be fully persuaded in
--, diseased, minister to a
--'s eye, Horatio
--, farewell the tranquil
--, out of, out of sight
--, musing in his sullein
--is its own place
--, men talk only to conceal their
--, gives to her, what he steals from her youth
--forbids to crave
--, she had a frugal
--, how fleet is a glance of the
--to mind
--, magic of the
--, Meccas of the
Minds, innocent and quiet
Minds are not ever craving
Mine own, do what I will with
Minister, one fair spirit for my
Minnows, Triton of the
Miracle instead of wit
Mirror up to nature
Mirth, within the limit of becoming
--grew fast and furious
Miserable have no other medicine
Miseries, in shallows and in
Misery acquaints a man with strange bed-fellows
--, steeped to the lips in
Misery's darkest cavern

--, happy he with such a
Moths, maidens like
Motley is the only wear
Mould, mortal mixture of earth's
Mountain tops, misty
--, robes the
--waves, her march is o'er the
Mountains interposed make enemies
--, Greenland's icy
Mourning, the oil of joy for
Mouth, out of thine own
--, gift horse in the
--, put an enemy in their
Muck, run a
Multitude of counselors
Murder, one, makes a villain
Murmurs, hollow, died away
Music the food of love
--, never merry when I hear
--, the man that hath no
--, discourse most excellent
--of her face
--hath charms to soothe
--, heavenly maid
--, sphere-descended maid
--, his very foot has
Music's golden tongue
Musical as is Apollo's lute
Muttons, to return to our
Myself, awe of such a thing as I
Mystery, burden of the
--of mysteries
Myrtle, cypress and

Naiad or a grace
Name, deed without a
--, what's in a
--, filches from me my good
--, mark the marble with his
--, at which the world grew pale
--, the magic of a
--, Phoebus, what a
Names, one of the few immortal
Narcissa's last words
Nathan said to David
Nation exalted by righteousness
--, a small one a strong
--, noble and puissant
Nations are as a drop of a bucket
--, mountains make enemies of
Native and to the manner born
--wood-notes wild
Nature's own sweet cunning hand
--'s soft nurse
--, one touch of
--might stand up
--, hold the mirror up to
--'s journeymen had made men
--could no farther go
--'s chief masterpiece
--made thee to temper man
--'s walks
--up to nature's God
--, extremes in
--to advantage dressed
--'s sweet restorer

--, who can paint like
--, mute, mourns when the poet dies
--'s teachings
--, sullenness against
--'s cockloft empty
--never did betray the heart that loved her
Nazareth, can any good come out of
Necessity, to make a virtue of
Need, deserted at his utmost
Needful, one thing is
Needle, true as the
Nests, birds of the air have
--, no birds in last year's
Nettle, tender-handed stroke a
News, first bringer of unwelcome
Night, I have passed a miserable
--, the very witching time of
--, ye meaner beauties of the
--, silver lining on the
--, day brought back my
--hideous
--, beauty like the
--, azure robe of
Nightingale was mute
Nights are wholesome
Niobe, all tears
--of nations
Ninny, Handel's but a
No pent-up Utica
No hammers fell
Nobility, betwixt the wind and his
Nods and becks
North, unripened beauties of the

Norval, my name is
Not she with traitorous kiss
Notes by distance
--, a duel's amang ye takin'
Nothing, an infinite deal of
--if not critical
Notion, foolish
Numbers, divinity in odd
Nun, the holy time is quiet as a
Nutmeg-graters, be rough as
Nymph, in thy orisons
Nympholepsy of some fond despair

Observance, the breach than the
Observed of all observers
Ocean, deep bosom of the
--, a painted
Odd numbers, divinity in
Odious, comparisons are
Odorous, comparisons are
Off with his head
Offense is rank
Offending, head and front of my
Office, hath but a losing
Officer, fear each bush an
Offspring of Heaven first-born
Oil, consumed the midnight
Old man eloquent
--Grimes is dead
Oliver, Rowland for an
Omega, Alpha and
One that hath, unto every
--kind kiss before we part

--, a stranger yet to
Pains, pleasure ill poetic
Painting, more than, can express
Pale, prithee, why so
Palinurus nodded
Palm, bear thy, alone
--, like some tall
Palpable, clothing the
Pangs of guilty power
Pantaloon, lean and slippered
Paradise of fools
--, walked in
Parallel, none but himself can be his
Parent of good
Parish church, plain as way to
Parting' in such sweet sorrow
Partitions thin their bounds divide
Party, gave up to, what was meant for mankind
Passing fair, is she not
Passion, till our, dies
--, the ruling
Passions fly with life
Pastures lie down in green
--, and fresh fields
Patches, a king of shreds and
Patience on a monument
Peace, all her paths are
--, piping times of
Peace and rest can never dwell
--, makes a solitude and calls it
--hath her victories
Pearls before swine
--did grow, how

--, who would search for
Pearls at random strung
Peasantry, a bold
Pebbles, as gathering
Pen of a ready writer
--, make thee famous by my
--dropped from an angel's wing
--mightier than the sword
Pendulum, man, thou
Pensioner, a miser's
People, thy, shall be my
Perdition catch my soul
Peril in thine eye
Perilous edge of battle
Perjuries, Jove laughs at lover's
Persuaded, lit every man be fully
Persons, no respect of
Petticoat, feet beneath her
Phalanx, in perfect
Phantasma, like a
Phantoms of hope
Philistines be upon thee
Philosopher that could bear the toothache
Philosophy, hast any, in thee
--, adversity's sweet milk
--, dreamt of in your
--, divine, charming is
--. in the calm light of mild
--, teaching by examples
Physic to the dogs
--, take
Physician, is there no
--, heal thyself

Picture, look here upon this
Pierian spring
Pigmies are pigmies still
Pigmy body, fretted the, to decay
Pigs squeak, as naturally as
Pilgrim shrines, such graves are
Pilot of the Galilean lake
Pinch, a hungry, lean-faced villain
Pink of courtesy
Pines, silent sea of
Pin's fee, set my life at a
Pitch, he that toucheth
Pitcher be broken
Pitiful, 't was wondrous
Pity, he hath a tear for
--'t is, 't is true
--, challenge double
--melts the mind to love
--'s akin to love
--gave ere charity began
--the sorrows of a poor old man
Place, jolly, in times of old
Places, lines in pleasant
Plan, not without a
--, the simple
Plato, thou reasonest well
Play's the thing
--, as good as a
Playmates I have had
Pleasantness, her ways are ways of
Pleased, I would do what I
Pleasure of being cheated
Pleasure, sweet is after pain

--in being mad
--at the helm
--with reason mixed
--in poetic pains
Pleasures, dance attendance on
Plowshares, swords into
Poet's eye in a fine frenzy
--'s pen turns them to shape
--soaring in the high reason of his fancy
Poetic pains, there is a pleasure in
Poetical, I would the gods had made thee
Poets in three distant ages
--intellible forms of
Pole, true as the needle to the
Pomp, take physic
--, lick absurd
Poor always ye have
--, simple annals of the
--, laws grind the
Pope of Rome, more than the
Poppies, pleasures are like
Poppy nor mandragora
Porcelain clay of humankind
Porcupine, like quills upon the fretful
Pot, death in the
Poverty, not my will, consents
--, steep me in
--, depressed, slow rises worth by
Power, take, who have the
Powers that be, ordained of God
Prague's proud arch
Praise, the garments of
--, damn with faint

--, solid pudding against empty
--all his pleasure
--, blame, love
--, none named thee but to
--undeserved
Praising what is lost
Pray, remained to
Prayer, whenever God erects a house of
--all his, business
--, the imperfect offices of
Preached as never to preach again
Precept upon precept
Preparation, dreadful note of
Prevaricate, Ralpho, thou dost
Priam's curtains
Pricks, hard to kick against the
Pride goeth before destruction
--fell with my fortunes
--and haughtiness of soul
--in their port
--that licks the dust
--, soul that perished in his
--, blend our pleasure or
--that apes humility
Primrose, sweet as the
Primrose, was to him a yellow
Princedoms, virtue's powers
Princes, sweet aspect of
Print, pleasant to see one's name in
Prior, what once was Matthew
Prison make, stone walls do not a
Procrastination is the thief of time
Prologues, happy, to the swelling act

Promise, keep the word of
Proof, give me ocular
Proofs of holy writ
Prophet not without honor
Prophets, pervert the
Propriety, frights the isle from her
Prove all things
Proverb and a by-word
Providence their guide
Prow, youth at the
Prunella, leather or
Psalms, purloin the
Punishment greater than I can bear
Pure, all things pure to the
Purpose, infirm of
--, nighty, never is o'ertook
Purse, who steals my, steals trash
Pyramids in vales

Quality, a taste of your
Quarrel, sudden and quick, in
Quarrel, that hath his, just
Question, that is the
Quickly, well it were done
Quiet, rural
Quips and cranks
Quivers, the Devil hath not in his

Race, not to the swift
--, boast a generous
--is rim, I bow to that whose
--, forget the human
--, rear my dusky

--of other days
Rachel weeping for her children
Rack, leave not a, behind
Rage, could swell the soul to
Raggedness, looped and windowed
Rags, the man forget not in
Rain from heaven droppeth
Rainbow, add another hue unto the
Rake, woman is at heart a
Ralph to Cynthia howls
Rank is but the guinea's stamp
Rat, I smell a
Rattle, pleased with a
Ravens, He that feedeth the
Ravishment, divine, enchanting
Ray, tints to-morrow with prophetic
Read, mark, learn
Reap, as you sow, y' are like to
Reason, no other but a woman's
--upon compulsion
--noble and most sovereign
--for my rhyme
--, make the worse appear the better
--, the feast of
--with pleasure mixed
Reasons are as two grains of wheat
Reckoning, so comes a
Red spirits and pay
Redeemer liveth, my
Religion, humanities of
Remember such things were
Remorse, farewell
Remote from men

--, unfriended
Reputation, seeking the bubble
--dies at every word
Resignation slopes the way
Resolution, native hue of
Retirement urges sweet return
Retreat, loopholes of
Reveals while she hides
Revelry, there was a sound of
Revels now are ended
Rhetoric, ope his mouth for
Rhine, wash the river
Rhyme nor reason
--, and build the lofty
--the rudder is
--, one for sense and one for
Rhyme, dock the tail of
Rialto, on the
Ribbon, give me what this, bound
Rich man and the camel
--, not gaudy
--with forty pounds a year
Richard is himself again
Riches, make themselves wings
Ridiculous and the sublime
Right, whatever is, is
Righteous forsaken
--overmuch
Righteousness and peace
--exalteth a nation
Ripe and ripe
Road, a rough, a weary
Roam, where'er I

Robbed, lie that is
Robbing Peter he paid Paul
Hobes and furred gowns hide all
Rocket, rose like a
Rod, and thy staff
--, a chief's a
--of empire
--, spare the
Roderick, art them a friend to
Rogue, every inch not fool is
Roman, than such a
--senate long debate
Romans, countrymen, and lovers
Rome, palmy state of
--, more than the Pope of
Romeo, wherefore art thou
Ronne, to waite, to ride, to
Room, ample, and verge enough
--, who sweeps a
Root, the axe is laid to the
Rose, happier is the, distilled
--by any other name
--in aromatic pain
--fairest when budding
Rosebuds, gather ye
Roses, the scent of the
Ross, the man of
Rot and rot
Rowland for an Oliver
Rub, ay, there's the
Rubies, wisdom priced above
--, where grew the
Ruin or to rule the state

--upon ruin
--, beauteous, lovely in death
Rule thee with a rod of iron
--, eye sublime declared absolute
--, the good old
Run, that he may, that readeth
Runs, who, may read
Rural quiet
Rustic moralist

Sadder and a wiser man
Sage, lie thought as a
Sail, set every threadbare
Saint, 't would provoke a
St. John mingles with my bowl
Saints in crape and lawn
--, his soul is with the
Salt of the earth
Samson, the Philistines be upon thee
Satan, get thee behind me
Satire's my weapon
--in disguise
Saul and Jonathan, undivided in death
Savage, wild in woods, the noble
Saviour's, the, birth is celebrated
Scars, he jests at
Sceptre, a barren, in my gripe
Schemes, best laid
School, the village master taught his little
Science, O star-eyed
Scoff, came to
Scorn, he will laugh thee to
--, what a deal of, looks beautiful

--, fixed figure, for the time of
--, laughed his word to
Scraps of learning dote, on
Screw your courage
Scripture, the Devil can cite
Scylla, your father
Sea, light that never was on
--, mysterious union with the
--, first that burst into that
Sea, alone, alone, on a wide
--, like ships that have gone down at
--, glad waters of the dark blue
--, the open
Seals of love
Second childishness
Sect, slave to no
See oursel's as others see us
Seek and ye shall find
Seems, madam, I know not
Self-slaughter, canon 'gainst
Sensations sweet
Sense, one for
--, want of decency is want of
Sentiment, pluck the eye of
Sepulchres, whited
Sermons in stones
Serpent sting thee twice
Serpents, be ye wise as
Servant can make drudgery divine
Service, I have done the state some
Servitude, base laws of
Shade, sitting in a pleasant
--, a more welcome

--, ah, pleasing
--, softening into shade
--, boundless contiguity of
--of that which once was great
Shadow, life is but a walking
Shadow, float double, swan and
Shadows come like
--, coming events cast their, before
Shaft that made him die
--at random sent
Shakespeare, sweetest, Fancy's child
Shall I, wasting in despair
Shame, an erring sister's
--, blush of maiden
Shape, take any, but that
--, thou com'st in such a questionable
--, execrable
--, if shape it might be called
Shapes and beckoning shadows
She walks in beauty
Shears, Fury with the abhorred
Shell, convolutions of a
--, music slumbers in the
Shepherd, habt any philosophy in thee
Sheridan, broke the die in moulding
Ship, idle as a painted
Ships that have gone down at sea
--that sailed for sunny isles
Shocks, the thousand natural
Shoe has power to wound
Shoot, to teach the young idea how to
Shore, rapture on the lonely
--, dull, tame

Show, that within which passeth
--, a driveller and a
Shrewsbury clock, fought a long hour by
Should auld acquaintance
Shrine of the mighty
Shut, shut the door
Sigh, passing tribute of a
--no more, ladies
Sighed and looked again
--unutterable things
Sign, dies and makes no
Sight, out of, out of mind
--, loved not at first
Seigniors, grave and reverend
Silence is the perfectest herald of joy
--in love bewrays more woe
--, ye wolves
--, come then, expressive
Siloa's brook
Simplicity a child
Sin, fools make a mock at
--of the world
--, wages of, is death
--, no, for a man to labor in his vocation
Single blessedness
Sinned against, more
Sinning, more sinned against than
Sins, charity shall cover the multitude of
Sion hill delight thee more
Sires, few sons attain the praise of their
Sires, green graves of your
Sirups, drowsy, of the world
Six hundred pounds a year

Sixpence, I give thee
Skies, looks commencing with the
--, raised a mortal to the
Skill, is but a barbarous
Sky, forehead of the morning
--, the storm that howl along the
--, souls are ripened in our northern
--, star sinning in the
--, canopied by the blue
Slain, thrice he slew the
Slaughter, lamb to the
--forbade to wade through
Slave, base is the, that pays
Slavery or death, which to choose
--a bitter draught
Slaves, what can ennoble
-, Britons never will be
Sleep, he giveth his beloved
--of a laboring man
--, folding the hands to
--, our life is rounded with a
--knits up the raveled sleave of care
--, gentle sleep
--, some must watch, while some must
--, tired nature's sweet restorer, balmy
Sleep, undisturbed
--, blessings on him who invented
--, the mantle that covers all human thought
Sleeve, wear my heart upon my
Slept, thought her dying when she
Sloth finds the down pillow hard
Slough of despond
Sluggard, 't is the voice of the

Slumber, a little
Small Latin and less Greek
--things compared with great
Smell, ancient and fish like
Smels, throwe her swete, al around
Smile that glowed celestial
--, to share the good man's
Smiles, seldom he
--, kisses, tears, and
Snails, her pretty feet, like
Snake, we hat'e scotched the
--like a wounded
Sneer, without sneering
--, laughing devil in his
Snow whiter than the driven
Snug as a bug
Society where none intrudes
Soldier full of strange oaths
Solid men of Boston
Solitude is sometimes but society
--, how passing sweet is
--, where are thy charms
--, inward eye of
--, makes a, and calls it peace
Something too much of this
Son of his own works
Song of Percy and Douglass
Sophonisba, O
Sorrow, pluck from the memory a rooted
--, wear a golden
--, parting is such sweet
--, to pine with feare and
--, her rent is

Source of sympathetic tears
South, o'er my ear like the sweet
Sow, wrong, by the ear
Soweth, shall reap, as he
Space and time annihilate
Spare the rod
Sparks fly upward
Sparrow, caters for the
--, providence in the fall of a
--, fall, or hero perish
Speak of me as I am
Spears into pruning-hooks
Speculation in those eyes
Speech, thought deeper than
Speed the going guest
--the parting guest
Spenser, renowned
Spin, nor toil not
Spirit wounded
--, haughty
--return unto God
--indeed is willing
--, present in
--stirring drum
--of my dream
--or more welcome shade
Spiriting, do my, gently
Spirits are not finely touched
--from the vasty deep
--twain
Spite,-in learned doctors
Splenetive and rash
Spoken at random

Sponge, drink no more than a
Spot is cursed, the
Springes to catch woodcocks
Spur to pride the sides of my intent
Squeak as naturally as pigs
Stage, where every man must play
--, all the world's n
--, struts and frets his hour upon the
--, the wonder of our
--, veteran on the
--, poor, degraded
Stale, flat, and unprofitable
Stand and wait
Stanley, on
Stanza, who pens a
Star, love a bright, particular
--, thy soul was like a
--, stay the morning
Stars, shooting, attend
--hide their diminished heads
--, battlements bore
Starts, everything by
State, a pillar of
--, what constitutes a
Statue that enchants the world
Stealth, do good by
Steed, farewell the neighing
Steel, though locked up in
--, my man 's as true as
--, grapple with hooks of
Sticking place, screw your courage to the
Still to be neat
--achieving, still pursuing

Sting, O death, where is thy
Stir, the fretful
Stoicism, the Romans call it
Stolen, not wanting what is
Stomach's sake, a little wine for the
Stone, fling but a
--, underneath this, doth lie
--, we raised not a
Stones, sermons in
--prate of my whereabouts
--of Rome
Stories, long, dull, and old
Storm, pelting of this pitiless
--, directs the
Storms of life, rainbow to the
Story, I have none to tell
Strange, 't was passing
Strangers, to entertain
--, by, honored
Straw, tickled with a
Streets, a lion is in the
--, squeak and gibber in the
Strength, king's name is a tower of
--, lovely in your
Strife, dare the elements to
Striving to better
Strong, battle not to the
--upon the stronger side
--without rage
Studies, still air of delightful
Study, much, is weariness
Stuff as dreams are made of
--, ambition 's made of sterner

Sublime, to suffer and be strong
--and the ridiculous
Success, 't is not in mortals to command
Suffer, how sublime to
Sufferance is the badge
Suffering ended with the day
--, child of
Suing long to bide
Sullenness against nature
Sum of more, giving thy
Summer, made glorious
--of your youth
Summons, upon a fearful
Summits, clad in colors of the air
Sun, no new thing under the
--of righteousness arise
--let not the, go down upon, your wrath
--, doubt the, doth move
--goes round, take all the rest the
--, benighted walks under the midday
--, as the dial to the
--, farthing candle to the
--, hail the rising
--, hold their glimmering taper to the
--. world without a
Sunday shines no Sabbath day
Sunlight drinketh dew
Sunshine made, and in the shady place
Suspicion haunts the guilty mind
Swan on St. Mary's lake
--, sweet, of Avon
Sweet, so coldly
Sweet day, so cool, so calm

Tam was glorious
Taste of your quality
Tear, some melodious
--, he gave to misery a
--in her eye
--, betwixt a smile and
--, every woe can claim
Tears, if you have
--such as angels weep
Tears, iron, down Plato's cheek
--sacred source of
--, baptized in
--, too deep for
--, flattered to
--from despair
--, idle tears
Temple, nothing ill can dwell in such a
Temples, groves were God's first
Tenderly, take her up
Tenor, noiseless, of their way
Terror, there is no, in your threats
Text, a rivulet of
That it should come to this
Theban, talk with this learned
There, 't is neither here nor
Thespis, the first professor of our art
Thetis, lap of
They conquer love that run away
Thick and thin, to dash through
Thief in the night, will come as a
--doth 'fear each bush
Thing, acting of a dreadful
--, never says a foolish

Things left undone
--, unutterable
--, God's sons are
Think too little, and talk too much
--those that, must govern
Thinks most, lives most
Thorn, withering on the virgin
Thou art the man
Thought, thy wish was father of that
--sicklied o'er with the pale cast of
--, would almost say her body
--, armor is his honest
--, whistled for want of
--, too much thinking to have common
--, not, one immoral
--, the dome of
--, the power of
--, deeper than speech
Thoughts, a dark soul and foul
--that breathe
--too deep for tears
--, great
Thousand, one shall become a
Thread of his verbosity
Thrift, thrift, Horatio
--may follow fawning
Thrones, dominations
Throng the lowest of your
Thumbs, by the pricking of my
Thunder, lightning, or in rain
Thwack, with many a stiff
Thyme, whereon the wild, grows
Tide in the affairs of men

Tidings, dismal, when he frowned
Tie, the silken
Tilt at all I meet
Timber, seasoned, never gives
Time and the hour
--, to the last syllable of recorded
--so hallowed and gracious
--, not of an age, but for all
--shall throw a dart at thee
--, how small a part of
--, with thee conversing, I forgot all
--, what will it not subdue
--'s noblest offspring
--, we take no note of
--toiled after him in vain
--adds increase to her truth
--has not cropt the roses
--, noiseless foot of
--count by heart-throbs
--, footprints on the band of
--has laid his hand gently
--, break the legs of
Times that try men's souls
Tinkling symbols
Toad, ugly and venomous
To be or not to be
To-day, be wise
Toe, on the light fantastic
Toil, envy, want the jail
--, those who think must govern those who
--and trouble, why all this
Tolerable and not to be endured
Tomb of him who would have made glad the world

Tombs, hark from the
To-morrow, boast not thyself of
--and to-morrow
--, do thy worst
--, already walks
Tongue, braggart with my
--let the canded
--that Shakespeare spake
--, music's golden
Tongues in trees
Too late I stayed
Tooth for tooth
--sharper than a serpent's
Toothache, philosopher that could endure the
Torrent of a woman's will
--, roll darkling down the
--, and whirlwind's roar
Torrents, motionless
Touch not, taste not
--harmonious
Towered cities please us
Towers, the cloud-capt
Trade's proud empire
Train up a child
Train, a melancholy
Traitors, our doubts are
Traps, Cupid kills with
Tray, Blanch, and Sweetheart
Treasure is, your heart will be where your
Tree, like a green bay
--is known by his fruit
Tree's inclined, as the twig is bent
--of deepest root is found

Trees, tongues in
Tribe, the badge of our
--, richer than all his
Trick worth two of that
Tricks, fantastic
Tried, she is to blame who has been
Trifles light as air
Triton of the minnows
Troop, farewell the plumed
Trope, out there flew a
Trouble, war, he sung, is toil and
Troubles, arms against a sea of
Trowel, laid on with a
Troy, half his, was burned
--, fired another
True so sad, so tender, and so
Truth, doubt, to be a liar
--in every shepherd's tongue
--from pole to pole
--, whispering tongues can poison
--crushed to earth
--, bright countenance of
Turf, green be the
Tweedledum and Tweedledee
Twilight gray, in sober livery
Two strings to his bow
Type of the wise

Unadorned, adorned the most
Unanimity is wonderful
Uncertain, coy, and hard to please
Uncle, O my prophetic soul I my
Underneath this stone doth lie

--sable hearse
Uneasy lies the head
Unfit, for all things
Unfortunate, one more
Unity, to dwell together in
Universe, born for the
Unknown, too early seen
--, argues yourselves
Unseen, born to blush
Unwept, unhonored and unsung
Unwhipped of justice
Uses, to what base
Utterance of the early gods
Utica, no pent-up

Vale of life
--, meanest floweret of the
Valiant taste of death but once
Vallombrosa, leaves that strew the brooks in
Valor, discretion the better part
--is oozing out
Vanity and vexation of spirit
Vanity of vanities
Variety, her infinite
--'s the spice of life
Vase, you may shatter the
Vault, the deep, damp
--, fretted
Vaulting ambition
Vein, I am not in the
Venice, I stood in
Verbosity, thread of his
Verge enough

Vernal seasons of the year
Verse, married to immortal
--, wisdom married to immortal
Verses, for rhyme the rudder is
Veteran, superfluous lags the
Vice, when, prevails
--is a monster
Vices, small
--, our pleasant
Vienna, looker-on here at
Victims, the little, play
Victorious o'er all the ills of life
View, when will the landscape tire the
Village master taught
Villain, one murder makes a
Violet, nodding grows
--, throw a perfume on the
--by a mossy stone
Violets, breathes upon a bank of
--plucked ne'er grow again
Virtue of necessity
--, assume a
--is her own reward
--alone is happiness
--makes the bliss
--, homage that vice pays to
Virtue linked with one
Virtues, we write in water
--, be to her, very kind
Virtuous, dost think because thou art
Visage, on his bold
Visible, darkness
Vision, write the, and make it plain

--, baseless fabric of a
--and faculty divine
Visits, like angel's
--like those of angels
Vocation, 't is my
Voice, a still, small
--, I hear a, you cannot
--of nature cries from the tomb
--in my dreaming ear melted
Voices, earth with her thousand
Void, have left an aching
Volume, within that awful
Vote that shakes the turrets of the land
Voyage of their life

Waist, hands round the slight
Wait, they also serve who stand and
Walk while ye have the light
--of virtuous life
Wall, weakest goes to the
Want lonely, retired to die
Wanting, art found
War, let slip the dogs of
--is toil and trouble
War, then was the tug of
--, my voice is still for
--to the knife
Warble his native wood-notes
Warriors feel, stern joy which
Watch and pray
Watches, our judgments as our
Water, unstable as
--, leadeth me beside the still

--, drink no longer
--, smooth runs the
--, the conscious, saw its God
--everywhere
Waters, cast thy bread upon the
--, the hell of
--, she walks the
Wave o' the sea
Waves, here shall thy proud, be stayed
Way of life, fallen into the sear and yellow leaf
--, noiseless tenor of their
Way, amend your
--of God are just
--, untrodden
We watched her breathing
Weakest goes to the wall
Weariness can snore upon the flint
Wearisome condition of humanity
Weep no more, lady
Well, not so deep as a
--, not wisely, but too
--of English undefyled
Westward the course of empire
Whale, very like a
What care I how fair she be
--, he knew what's
Whatever is, is right
Wheel broken at the cistern
--, who breaks a butterfly upon a
When shall we three meet again
Whereabout, prate of my
Wherefore, for every why he had a
Whining schoolboy

Whip, in every honest hand a
Whirlwind, they shall reap the
--, ride in the
Whispering lovers made
--will ne'er consent
Whispers of fancy
Whistle, clear as a
Whistled as he went
Whither thou goest I will go
Who builds a church to God
--runs may read
Wicked cease from troubling
--flee when no man pursueth
Wife, you are my true and honorable
--and children impediments to great enterprises
Wiles, simple
Will, he that complies against his
Will turn the current of a woman's
--, if she will
Willows, hanged our harps on the
Win, they laugh that
Wind, did fly on the wings of the
--, they have sown the
--bloweth us it listeth
--, sits the, in that corner
--, as large a charter as the
--, blow, thou winter
--, blow, come wrack
--and his nobility
--, idle, as the
--, blow and crack your cheeks
--. ill, turns none to good
--, shrink from sorrow's keenest

--, give the, the lie
--was all before them
--, look round the habitable
--, so stands the statue that enchants the
--'s dread laugh
--, unintelligible
--, fever of the
--too much with us
--, I have not loved the
--falls, when Rome falls
--knows nothing of its greatest men
World's wide enough for thee and me
Worlds, mine arm should conquer twenty
--, wreck of matter and the crush of
--, exhausted, and imagined new
--, allured to brighter
Worm dieth not
Worms have eaten them
Worse, greater feeling to the
Worship God, he says
Worth, conscience of her
--, what is, in anything
--by poverty depressed
--makes the man
--, sad relic of departed
Wound, he jests at scars that never felt a
Wrack, blow wind, come
Wrath, soft answer turneth away
--, let not the sun go down upon your
--, nursing her, to keep it warm
Wreck of matter
Wretches, poor naked
--, feel what, feel

--hang that jurymen may dine
Writ, and what is, is writ
Writer, pen of a ready
Writing, true ease in
Wrong, always in the
Wrongs unredressed
Year, starry girdle of the
--, saddest days of the
Years, we spend our
--, love of life increased with
Years, dim with the mist of
--, live in deeds, not
Yesterdays have lighted fools
Yorick! alas poor
York, this sun of
Young, and now am old
--, when my bosom was
--, and both were
Yours, as if her merit lessened
Youth, remember thy Creator
--in the morn and liquid dew
--at the prow
--, gives to her mind what he steals from her
--to fortune and to lame unknown
--of labor, with an age of ease
--, friends in